DEADLIER THAN THE MALE

Fargo figured Cassandra was falling for him or at least his story. But she didn't lower her shotgun. Instead she scooped up a pistol and fired two shots into the floor.

Men poured into the room. "Come on, you peckerwoods!" the ravishing redhead bawled.

Punches rained down on Fargo. Kicks slammed into his sides. He fought as best he could, landing blows to the right and left. He saw a kneecap and slammed a heel into it. But knuckles raked his face. A fist plowed into his stomach. Dimly he heard Cassandra voice, "Pin him down! Tie him up!"

Minutes later, the Trailsman lay hog-tied on the floor. Cassandra checked the bonds to make sure they couldn't be broken. Then she told the men to leave.

She smiled at Fargo. "My brothers return tomorrow. 'Til then, I have you all to myself."

He read the look in her eyes. A chill ran through him. Normally he wouldn't worry about being alone with a lady. But this was no lady. This was a murderous maneater who could make death seem easy. . . .

THE
TRAILSMAN
158

TEXAS TERROR

by

Jon Sharpe

A SIGNET BOOK

SIGNET
Published by the Penguin Group
Penguin Books USA Inc., 375 Hudson Street,
New York, New York 10014, U.S.A.
Penguin Books Ltd, 27 Wrights Lane,
London W8 5TZ, England
Penguin Books Australia Ltd, Ringwood,
Victoria, Australia
Penguin Books Canada Ltd, 10 Alcorn Avenue,
Toronto, Ontario, Canada M4V 3B2
Penguin Books (N.Z.) Ltd, 182–190 Wairau Road,
Auckland 10, New Zealand

Penguin Books Ltd, Registered Offices:
Harmondsworth, Middlesex, England

First published by Signet, an imprint of Dutton Signet,
a division of Penguin Books USA Inc.

First Printing, February, 1995
10 9 8 7 6 5 4 3 2 1

Copyright © Jon Sharpe, 1995
All rights reserved

The first chapter of this book previously appeared in *Ghost Ranch Massacre*,
the one hundred fifty-seventh volume in this series.

 REGISTERED TRADEMARK—MARCA REGISTRADA

Printed in the United States of America

The Trailsman

Beginnings . . . they bend the tree and they mark the man. Skye Fargo was born when he was eighteen. Terror was his midwife, vengeance his first cry. Killing spawned Skye Fargo, ruthless, cold-blooded murder. Out of the acrid smoke of gunpowder still hanging in the air, he rose, cried out a promise never forgotten.

The Trailsman they began to call him all across the West: searcher, scout, hunter, the man who could see where others only looked, his skills for hire but not his soul, the man who lived each day to the fullest, yet trailed each tomorrow. Skye Fargo, the Trailsman, and the seeker who could take the wildness of a land and the wanting of a woman and make them his own.

1860 . . . deep in Texas,
where the sun is hotter,
the women wilder, and the killers
all have itchy trigger fingers. . . .

1

The small town of Ripclaw was just like any other in the state of Texas. Or so Skye Fargo thought as his weary pinto stallion plodded up the middle of the dusty main street. Few people were abroad in the blistering heat of the late afternoon. He saw an elderly couple come out of the general store and a pair of young women in tight-fitting dresses sashay toward a grimy saloon.

At the livery Fargo reined up. Easing his tired body to the ground, he pulled his heavy-caliber Sharps from its doeskin saddle scabbard and led the Ovaro into the cool interior. "Anybody here?" he called out.

From the murky shadows at the rear emerged a scarecrow of a man in patched overalls, a sliver of straw jutting from the corner of his thin mouth. Hooking his thumbs in frayed suspenders, he said, "Howdy, stranger. I'm Eli and I run the place. What can I do for you?"

"I'd like to put my horse up for the night," Fargo said, taking the stallion to an empty stall. "Give him some feed, some water, and a rubdown. I'll be by at first light."

"Sure thing, pardner," Eli said, leaning on a post while studying the pinto. "That's a right fine animal you've got there, if you don't mind my saying so. And I know, 'cause horseflesh is my stock and trade." He spat the straw out. "Looks like you've been on the go a spell."

"Two days," Fargo said. He didn't bother to mention it had been two days with little food and no sleep. "I saw a hotel on the way in. Is it worth staying at?"

"The Imperial? Shucks, yes. The lady who owns it prides herself on having a clean, upstanding establishment. I hear tell

9

she changes the bedding once a week, whether the beds need changing or not. And the food she serves is enough to make a single man want to dig in roots."

Fargo leaned his rifle against the stall and removed his bedroll and saddlebags. As he began stripping off his saddle, Eli came forward.

"No need to do that, mister. I can see you're plumb tuckered out. Leave the rig to me. I'll store it in the tack room till morning."

"Thanks." Fargo made for the double doors, draping the saddlebags over his right shoulder. Under his left arm went the bedroll. He was almost to the bright sunlight when the owner called out.

"In case my helper is here in the morning and not me, I'll need a name to tell him. "Who might you be?"

"Fargo."

"What?"

"Skye Fargo."

Striding into the harsh glare, Fargo thought he heard an odd gurgling sound and glanced back. Eli was as rigid as a board, his dark eyes as wide as walnuts. "Is anything wrong?" Fargo asked.

"No, sir!" Eli blurted. "Ain't nothing the matter at all! Had a lump in my throat, is all. You go on about your business and I'll tend to your pinto."

Fargo nodded, then made for the Imperial, his boots raising puffs of dust, his spurs jangling. He pulled his hat brim lower to shield his face. The only thing moving outside the hotel was a solitary fly, which he swatted aside as he gripped the door handle. About to go in, he happened to glance toward the stable and saw Eli bolting across the street as if the devil himself were in pursuit. Strange man, Fargo reflected.

The lobby was comfortably furnished. Potted plants, drapes, and doilies showed a woman's touch. Fargo crossed to the front desk and tapped the top of a small bell beside the register.

A curtain parted and out strolled a stunning brunette in a green frilly dress barely less revealing than those of the saloon girls. She blinked on seeing him, then smiled suggestively and

10

leaned on the countertop, showing more of her already ample cleavage. "Why, hello handsome. Haven't seen you around before. I'm Eleanor Seaver, but most folks call me Ellen."

"I'm told you have a fine hotel here," Fargo said, setting down his bedroll.

Ellen smirked. "Well, I don't mean to brag, but you won't find a cleaner, quieter place to stay between here and the Rio Grande."

Fargo placed an elbow in front of her and lowered his head until he stared directly at her gorgeous mounds. "It has other charms as well, I see. I think I'm going to enjoy my stay."

"I like to give my customers a personal touch you won't find anywhere else," Ellen said softly. "And a few lucky souls get special treatment."

"What does a man have to do to qualify?"

"Be good-looking," Ellen responded, then winked. "Damned good-looking, like you are."

"Lucky me."

"Here," Ellen said, spinning the book toward him. "Jot down your John Hancock and I'll fetch you a key."

Fargo felt her hand lightly brush his when she turned. He admired the saucy swirl to her slim hips as she went through the curtain. His manhood, long denied female company, twitched eagerly.

The ink in the well was nearly dry. Fargo had to poke the pen in a few times before he could finish his signature. Replacing it, he idly gazed through the sparkling front window and noticed Eli and two other men hurrying past, all three staring straight ahead so intently their necks seemed to be locked in place. What was that all about? he wondered. The rustle of smooth fabric on sheer stockings brought him around.

"Here you go, big man." Ellen handed over a key. "Room one twenty-one, the last one on the right. It's nice and peaceful back there. No one will disturb you."

"I'm hoping at least one person will come by," Fargo said, staring her right in the eyes.

A faint pink tinge capped both of Ellen's full cheeks. "You never know. Maybe someone will." She gave a little cough. "I know I have to drop by later. I cleaned your room yesterday and there was no towel over the washbasin."

"I could sure use one," Fargo admitted. "A long time on the trail makes a man whiffy."

"Personally," Ellen said, bending so close their noses nearly touched, "I like your scent just fine. Some men stink to high heaven, like they carry a polecat in their drawers. You sort of remind me of new leather."

"And that's good?"

"I *love* new leather."

Chuckling, Fargo hoisted his bedroll. "There's no rush on the towel," he commented. "I could use a nap before I do anything else."

"Oh?" Ellen sounded disappointed. "All right. I'll wait an hour or so. By then most everyone will be out eating supper. We'll likely have the whole hotel all to ourselves."

"You sure you'd be safe?" Fargo joked.

"Are you sure *you* would?" she countered.

Fargo walked to the hall. He had just entered when a low gasp drew his attention to the front desk, where Eleanor Seaver stood gaping at the countertop. "Are you all right?"

"Fine," Ellen said, vigorously bobbing her chin. "Just dandy. You go get that sleep. I'll be along later like I promised."

The room was close to the rear exit. Fargo had seen plusher accommodations, but few as nicely arranged. He leaned the rifle in a corner, tossed his gear on the chair, and stepped to the sole window. It fronted an alley partially filled with old boxes and empty crates. He raised the sill a few inches to admit fresh air, then lay on his back on the bed, careful not to rake the spread with his spurs.

For the better part of an hour, Fargo tried to doze off. Given his fatigue and the interval since he'd last slept, he figured he would have no problem. But a vague feeling of unease gnawed at the back of his mind, making him toss and turn from one side to the next. He assumed it must have something to do with his current job.

A rich businessman in Waco had offered Fargo a hefty sum to track down the pair of killers responsible for the death of the businessman's son. Ordinarily, Fargo didn't hire himself out as a bounty hunter, but in this case he had made an exception. For two reasons.

First, the man in Waco was a kindly old-timer, his wife of the same mold. Everyone Fargo had talked to in Waco made the same claim. The couple were the kind who would do anything for anyone, and had. They'd reared their son to be the same way. The boy had been their pride and joy, and his murder had left them devastated.

Second, the killing itself had been particularly vicious. Two men had broken into the store and were rifling the safe when they were caught in the act by the son. They'd tied him to a chair, stuffed a gag in his mouth, and pistol-whipped him so badly every bone in his face had been broken. Not satisfied there, they had kicked and stomped on him until all his ribs were busted, his arms and legs broken, and his internal organs too severely damaged to ever heal. The son had died several days later.

Fargo had been passing through Waco after a short stay in Mexico. Somehow word had gotten to the couple, who had promptly paid him a visit and pleaded for his help. He didn't like to think he was growing soft, but the old woman's tears had touched him deeply. So he'd accepted.

Learning the identities of the two killers had been easy. After pocketing their loot, the pair had brazenly walked out the front door to their horses, mounted, and headed out of town, pausing only once to shoot to ribbons a wanted poster nailed to a pole. It had been a wanted poster of *them*.

Frank and Bob Jeffers were known from one end of Texas to the other as the most cold-blooded badmen ever born. Their string of savage killings went back some ten years, and nothing the Rangers or local law officers had done in all that time had been able to put a crimp in their lawless ways.

In this instance, the marshal of Waco had formed a posse and chased the pair to the limits of his jurisdiction. Later, special Rangers had been sent in, but the trail had grown cold, the clues had dried up. The Jefferses had disappeared once again.

Fargo would be the first to admit he had little hope of finding the vermin. He was a tracker, not a lawman. Give him fresh tracks and he could follow anyone anywhere. But he'd given his word to the Walkers. He'd try his best for two weeks. If he came up empty-handed, he'd send them a wire and head north for Denver.

Now Fargo had only four days to go. He'd followed up lead after lead without result. The latest information, gleaned from a faro dealer in the last town, was that one Jeffers had been seen heading north across the Black Prairie. Which explained Fargo's presence in Ripclaw, but not why he couldn't sleep.

Sitting up, Fargo went to the basin and splashed water on his face and neck. Since he couldn't rest, he figured he might as well make himself presentable for when Ellen dropped by. As he turned off the spigot, his keen ears registered a faint scraping noise from out in the hallway.

Guessing it was the brunette, Fargo tiptoed to the door and positioned himself slightly behind it. He'd bid her enter, and when she did, scoop her into his arms. Women liked men who acted on the spur of the moment, who could surprise them, make them laugh. Besides, he wanted to get his hands on those melons of hers.

But Fargo was the one surprised. He had his eyes on the latch and was smirking in anticipation when he heard another noise, the raspy click of a pistol hammer being cocked. Then two more.

Twilight had claimed Ripclaw. In the room it was darker, so Fargo didn't bother hiding. Quickly, he grabbed the wooden chair and planted his feet firmly on the other side of the jamb, where he could see the door opening. Which it did, slowly, a moment later.

Fargo had his broad back flush to the wall. He saw the tip of a revolver barrel poke inside, then a hand, a thick wrist. The outline of a man's face appeared, swinging toward the bed as if the man knew right where it was located. The man took a step, edging inside, and that was when Fargo swung with all his might.

There was a tremendous crash as the chair caught the intruder flush in the face. The chair shattered. The man flew backwards into the corridor, his six-gun blasting once, sending a slug into the ceiling. Someone else cried out and there were two loud thuds.

Fargo slammed the door shut. He dashed to his rifle as the hotel echoed to three gunshots and the top panel in the door was splintered by three bullet holes. Spinning, he spotted a figure beyond the door. Fargo tucked the stock to his shoulder, took a hasty bead, and fired, the roar of the big Sharps near-deafening in the confines of the room.

In the hall someone cursed.

Someone else squawked, "Sweet Jesus! The son of a bitch has a cannon in there!"

"Hush, damn you!" snapped a third man, and a flurry of whispering erupted.

Fargo knew the local law would come running, but he didn't aim to stay there until that happened. Being trapped in the room made him edgy, gave him the same sort of feeling a cornered mountain lion or bear experienced when hemmed in by hunters. He needed room to move, to take the fight to those trying to take his life.

Darting to the window, Fargo eased it as high as it would go. He slipped a boot outside, lowered it to the bare earth. Bending, he eased his shoulders through and was straightening when a hard object jammed into his temple and a gruff voice snarled a warning in his ear.

"Make one more move, you bastard, and your brains will be splattered all over that wall!"

Usually, Fargo made it a point not to dispute a man holding him at gunpoint. But someone was trying to kick in the door, evidently in the belief he had locked it, and in another few moments the killers would break in and automatically throw lead in his direction. So it was either turn the tables or die, and Fargo had no intention of being planted in an unmarked grave on the boot hill of a two-bit town in the middle of nowhere.

The man with the rifle stepped partly into view and shifted his rifle lower. In that split second, Skye Fargo pivoted on his boot heel and spread the muzzle of the Sharps into the man's gut. The man screeched, doubling in torment, his rifle slipping from weakened fingers. Fargo rammed his rifle stock into the man's head and he dropped like a poled ox.

Half the door was gone. Fargo saw several black silhouettes forcing their way inside. He dived as a pistol cracked. The bullet struck the sill, missing him by a fraction. Hitting on his shoulder, Fargo rolled smoothly and shoved erect, palming his Colt as he rose and covering the window.

Suddenly, from the street, a new voice added to the racket. "Here he is! Down the alley! Come on, before he gets away!"

A rifle thundered. Fargo answered once, watched a figure leap around the corner. He whirled and ran, wondering just how many he was up against and where in the hell the marshal of Ripclaw had gotten to. Ten feet from the end of the alley, he drew up short. Another figure had appeared, blocking his path. Fargo detected the glint of metal and raised his Colt, taking deliberate aim. His target, though, took one look at him, screamed in terror, flung a rifle aside, and fled.

Not knowing what to make of the man's behavior, Fargo raced around the corner and stopped to reload the Sharps. At the rear of another building fifty feet to the right a gun cut loose, the shots chipping wood out of the wall behind him. Ducking, he cat-footed to the far side of the hotel.

In the main street men shouted, boots pounded. More yelling came from the alley Fargo had vacated. He shook his head in bewilderment, racking his brain for an explanation as to why a small army of gunmen was after him. So far as he knew, he had no enemies in that part of the country.

Further pondering was cut short by the arrival of another one, a skinny man holding a shotgun. Fargo swung the Sharps as the man lifted his weapon to fire. The stock of the rifle struck the barrel of the shotgun, deflecting it so that the buckshot ripped into the side of the next building. Fargo plowed a fist into the man's jaw and the man crumpled like so much paper.

The gunmen were closing in from all directions. Fargo sped along the side of the hotel, intending to lose himself in the crowd that was no doubt gathering out front. He was halfway there when several dark figures materialized ahead at the selfsame instant an open window beckoned on his left. Without hesitation, Fargo threw himself inside and landed on soft carpet. Rising into a crouch, he hugged the wall, listening as men ran past. Their footsteps slowed at the rear.

"I thought I saw him!"

"He must have gone back around!"

"Hank, is he over yonder?"

"No sign of him here."

"Look everywhere. He can't get away."

Working swiftly, Fargo closed and latched the window and moved into the dim recesses of the room. Upraised voices seemed to ring the hotel. Shadows flitted across the glass pane, and seconds later a man in a white hat stopped to peer in. Fargo trained his cocked Colt on the gunman's head, but the man moved on.

Relaxing a hair, Fargo stepped to the closed door. He tried the latch, found it unlocked. A considerable commotion had broken out, and a peek into the hallway showed why. Agitated guests milled about in excitement, demanding to know what all the shooting was about. Ellen moved among them, evidently reassuring them all was well.

Fargo shut the door before anyone noticed him. He threw the bolt, then sat in a rocking chair that faced the window. For the time being he was safe. A faint hint of musky perfume hung in the air, and he wondered if the last person to stay here had been a woman.

For the longest time the hunt went on. Fargo heard them shouting from one end of Ripclaw to the next. He marveled that no one stepped in to quell the disturbance and wished he knew exactly who was after him and why.

It was close to midnight when the uproar quieted. Fargo decided to try for his room. He'd reclaim his belongings, sneak to the livery, and go find a spot in the nearby woods where he could hole up for a while. His hand was closing on the bolt when he heard someone approach the door. Then the latch wriggled, rattling loudly as the person tried to force the door open. Silently, sliding the bolt, Fargo stepped aside.

Light bathed the carpet. The person entered, unsuspecting. Fargo glimpsed cascading dark hair as he pounced, looping his right arm around the woman's throat. "Don't cry out!" he warned. "I won't hurt you if you do as I say."

The woman had tensed and tried to tear free. On hearing his voice, she stopped, standing meekly. "I won't scream, Mr. Fargo, if that's what you're worried about."

Fargo closed the door with a shove of his foot, then walked around in front of Eleanor Seaver. She regarded him as a frightened doe might regard a stalking wolf. "I didn't know who it was," he said. "Sorry if I scared you."

"I'm fine," Ellen said nervously. She played with the frill on her dress a moment. "Pretty clever of you to hide right under their noses. They've been looking everywhere, and here you are in my own room."

"Who are they?" Fargo asked urgently. "Why do they want me so badly?"

"You don't know?"

Fargo shook his head.

"Marshal Lee Howes has deputized twenty men to bring you in dead or alive—preferably slung over a saddle. They say you're a dangerous character, a killer."

"They must have mistook me for someone else," Fargo said. "I'm not wanted anywhere."

"If you say so," Ellen responded skeptically.

"You don't believe me?"

"I'd like to. I truly would. But everyone knows about Kingfish."

Fargo was more confused than ever. Kingfish was the name of the last town he'd stopped at, the place where he'd been told by a faro dealer that one of those he sought had recently passed through. He'd immediately purchased a few supplies, saddled up, and rode out. Nothing else of any consequence had occurred. "What happened there?"

Ellen looked at him in disbelief. "You don't remember killing those people? Were you drunk at the time?"

"What people?" Fargo said, grasping her wrist in annoyance. He was fast losing his patience with the whole business and couldn't wait to get shy of Ripclaw.

"The evening before last a man calling himself Skye Fargo took a room at a small boardinghouse in Kingfish. Later that night he killed the owners and two boarders and lit a shuck for parts unknown." Ellen paused. "The sheriff sent a wire to our

18

town marshal. Marshal Howes told all the merchants in Ripclaw to be on the lookout for you."

Now Fargo understood the liveryman's reaction on hearing his name, and why Ellen had gasped when she saw his signature. "I'm not the hombre they want," he insisted. "I have to talk to your marshal and set things straight."

"I wouldn't try, if I were you," Ellen said. "He's liable to shoot you on sight."

Just then the door shook to the pounding of a heavy fist, and a deep voice bellowed, "It's the marshal! Open up! I know you're in there."

2

"Oh, my God!" Ellen said. "He's found you!" Hand over her mouth, she backed away.

Fargo was at the door in two bounds. Holding the Colt close to his chest, the Sharps at his side, he braced for the crash certain to come when the lawman and the deputies tried to break in. He didn't want to tangle with them, but if Ellen was right about them shooting him on sight, it wouldn't do him any good to try and talk his way out of the fix he was in.

"Come on, Ellen," the marshal coaxed. "I just need a minute of your time. I heard you talking to someone, so you can't pretend you're not in."

Fargo motioned for the brunette to do as the lawdog wanted, but Ellen balked, shaking her head in fright. He strode to her side, gripped her arm, and pulled her over.

"Ellen, damn it!" Howes snapped. "I don't have all night for this nonsense. I have a killer to find. I don't much care who you're seeing this week, but I need to see you."

The brunette gulped and licked her lips. Fargo prodded her with the Colt and nodded at the hall. She tried to speak, coughed, and tried again. "Just a moment," she croaked. Visibly struggling to compose herself, she reached for the latch, then cracked the door an inch. "Yes?"

"Listen, I'm truly sorry about barging in on you at a time like this," the marshal said, "but I wanted to let you know I'm taking Fargo's personal effects down to the jail. And don't fret your pretty head none about the damages to your place. Send me a bill and I'll make sure the council antes up the money."

From where Fargo stood, he couldn't see the lawman. He

watched Ellen's face for any hint of betrayal, but she was composed now and handled herself well.

"I don't know why you didn't wait until morning, Lee," she said. "You could have taken him into custody real easy when he walked out on the street."

"And run the risk of bystanders being hit?" Marshal Howes rejoined. "No, thank you, ma'am. I figure we did right by trying to snare him while he was in his room. How was I to know he has the ears of a cat and the reflexes to boot?"

"Do you have any idea where he is?"

"No. But his horse is still at the stable so we suspect he's hiding somewhere here in town. It's just a matter of time before we nail his hide to the wall."

Fargo heard the lawman turn and start to walk off. Judging by the heaviness of the steps, Howes was a big man.

"Lee?" Ellen said.

Suspecting a trick, Fargo sidled closer to her and touched her arm with the Colt. Not that he'd really harm her. But if she thought he would, she'd be less likely to give him away.

"Ma'am?"

"Is there any chance you're after the wrong man? Fargo didn't seem like a murderer to me."

"Haven't you heard the old saw about not judging a book by its cover? Maybe he doesn't look the part, but the fact is that an hombre with his name made wolf meat of four decent folks and then rode off like he didn't have a care in the world." Marshal Howes paused. "Don't let his kind fool you, Ellen. I've seen baby-faced kids who'd shoot their own mothers if the whim struck them." He departed saying, "Have a nice night."

Ellen slowly closed the door and turned. She swatted the Colt aside as if it were an annoying fly. "Quit pretending, mister. I don't care what he says, my intuition tells me I can trust you. You're no killer."

Fargo replaced the Colt in its holster and took a seat in the rocker. "I'm glad at least one person in Ripclaw is on my side."

"I was scared there for a bit," Ellen admitted, going to the bed. "But then I got to thinking. If you were the awful monster they make you out to be, you would have strangled me the moment I walked in the room to keep me from calling out."

"You'll help me, then?"

Ellen shrugged. "I don't see how I can be of any use, other than letting you stay in my room for the night."

"I'm obliged," Fargo said absently. He was thinking about Kingfish, and how to go about clearing his name. Surely someone there had seen the killer and would be able to vouch for the fact he wasn't the one.

"Are you hungry? I can go get some food."

"No, thanks," Fargo said. His appetite was gone, but not his fatigue. Now that the excitement had passed, the days without sleep were catching up with him. He fought off a yawn and shook his head to clear his thoughts.

"You're exhausted," Ellen commented. "Why don't you stretch out and I'll keep watch?"

Fargo glanced at her. Was she trustworthy, or would she run to the lawman as soon as he dozed off? "I'll sleep in a while," he hedged, to give himself time to make up his mind.

"As you wish." Ellen folded her hands in her lap and gnawed on her lower lip like an indecisive little girl. "I've never done anything like this before. Harbored a wanted man, I mean."

"That makes us even. I've never been a wanted man."

"Do you have any idea who really killed those poor people?"

"Not yet. But I aim to find out."

Ellen turned, fluffed a pillow, and swung her legs onto the edge of the bed so she could lean back. "Just in case you're wondering, Eli was the one who turned you in. Not me."

Fargo remembered seeing the stableman scurry across the street. "Should have known," he said. The sight of her lying there, looking so pretty and inviting with the dress molded to the contours of her luscious body, made his mouth go dry. He reminded himself that now was hardly the proper time or place to indulge his craving for female companionship.

"About Kingfish," she said. "Were you there about the time of the killings?"

"Yes," Fargo confessed. "Near as I can tell, I left town a

22

few hours before it happened."

"So maybe it's a simple case of mistaken identity."

"I hope so," Fargo said. Deep down, though, he had his doubts. It was too much of a coincidence to think the killer had plucked his name out of thin air. Whoever was responsible must have known he'd been there. He recollected all those he had talked to: the faro dealer, a bartender, the livery owner, and several women in a saloon. At no time had he mentioned his own name to any of them. He'd merely asked about Frank and Bob Jeffers.

"Do you know anyone who would want to frame you?" Ellen asked.

"No," Fargo said. The brothers were prime candidates, but they had no idea he was after them. Secrecy had been one of the conditions under which he'd accepted the job. Irritated by the turn of events and his inability to solve the riddle, Fargo rose and paced.

"You need to relax more, handsome."

Halting, Fargo admired her openly. The rhythm of her bosom rising and falling as she breathed and the swell of her shapely thighs under her dress were enough to send a tingle rippling through his loins. "Was that an invite?" he asked hoarsely.

"It was if you want it to be."

Fargo leaned the Sharps against the rocker, removed his spurs and boots, and sat next to her. Ellen stared up at him without fear. Taking her chin in his hand, he gently applied his lips to hers. Her mouth quivered a few seconds, then she responded, tentatively at first but with increasing ardor as his hands found her breasts and lightly massaged them. He lay down beside her, their bodies so close he could feel the heat hers radiated. She ran a hand through his hair, sending his hat toppling to the floor. Her other hand roamed his chest, his stomach.

Fargo kissed her throat, her ear. He licked the lobe and nibbled on the sensitive skin at the nape of her neck. Pressing his legs against hers, he ran a hand down her flat stomach to the junction of her thighs and cupped her womanhood. She

23

moaned, squirmed, and parted her legs to grant him freer access to her charms.

Ellen's skin smelled of lilacs. Fargo inhaled her fragrance as he lathered her throat with his tongue. Unfastening the back of her dress, he eased it off both arms, then exposed her gorgeous globes. The nipples were already hard, erect. Taking the tip of one in his mouth, he tweaked it, causing her to wriggle her bottom and dig her nails into his back.

"You're good, lover!" she said huskily.

Fargo squeezed and rubbed both breasts until they were warm to the touch and the slightest pressure made her pant. When he had both nipples good and hard, he dipped to her navel, swirling his tongue around inside of it. She giggled, pulled on his hair, and rubbed her legs against him.

A new, earthy scent replaced the lilacs. Fargo pried her undergarments aside to get at her core. The first contact set her backside to pumping convulsively. He had to take a firm grip and hold on tight as he nuzzled her passion spot. She humped against him, harder and harder, her hands gripping the back of his head. Between the motion of her hips and the smothering effect of her hands, he could scarcely breathe.

Fargo finally broke loose to kiss her silken inner thighs. He inserted a finger into her slit and was enfolded in her arms. She glued her soft lips to his, her tongue probing deep into his mouth. He stroked her, gently at first, then with increasing urgency. She bucked, bit, matched his thrusts with thrusts of her own.

When he judged the time right, Fargo removed his finger, unhitched his pants, and got onto his knees between her legs. She opened wide, grinning sensuously. Aligning his member, Fargo inserted the tip, coiled his legs, and drove into her like an elk in rut.

Ellen about flew off the bed. She yipped once, then bit her lip. Her head fell back, her mouth slackened, and she breathed in great puffs of hot air.

Fargo established a slow pace and stuck to it no matter how she enticed him to speed up. Her nails raked his back, her lips moistened every square inch of his face and neck. Only when her eyes rolled back and she drove her hips at him as if trying to pound him to a pulp did he match her frantic heavings and allow himself to near the summit.

The climax, when it came, was like the crest of a towering ocean wave. It swept Fargo along on a tide of physical pleasure. For minutes he coasted, adrift in the ecstasy of release, his heartbeat gradually returning to normal, his blood cooling.

Sleep claimed Fargo as he slid off Ellen onto his back. It was the sleep of total depletion. His dreams were fitful, and he remembered none of them. Of the real world he knew nothing at all, until the jab of a hard object into his stomach snapped him from dreamland into the reality of a living nightmare.

The first sight Fargo beheld was a great moon of a face covered with grizzle, a cigar wedged between lips like thick slabs. Under the face was a brown leather vest. Pinned to the vest was a shiny badge bearing a single word: MARSHAL.

The second sight Fargo saw were the half-dozen armed men with rifles pointed in his direction. They were uniformly grim, their expressions revealing more eloquently than words the fate in store for him if he gave them any trouble.

Last, Fargo saw Eleanor Seaver over by the door, arms clasped tight to her chest, tears rimming her eyes. She smiled and spoke before anyone else. "Don't be mad, Skye. I did this for your own good."

Fargo slowly raised his head and held his hands out from his sides. "My own good?" he repeated bitterly. His mouth felt filled with cobwebs.

"That's right," Ellen assured him. "I made Lee promise not to harm you if you'll go along peacefully. And he's as good as his word."

"True enough," growled the lawman, "but it wouldn't pain me any if you to act up so I could break my word with a clear conscience."

"Lee!" Ellen declared. She focused on Skye again. "Don't you see? I told him everything you told me and he vowed to look into it. If anyone can clear your name, it's him."

"You're a regular Good Samaritan," Fargo muttered, sitting up. He received a poke in the ribs that lanced him with pain.

"I'd keep a civil tongue, mister," Marshal Howes suggested. "If it'd been up to me, you'd be so full of lead right this minute I could mine you and make a mint." He lowered his rifle. "But I've known Ellen here a few years, and I know she has a good head on her shoulders. Since she thinks you just might be innocent, I'll give you the benefit of the doubt against my better judgment."

"I didn't kill those people," Fargo bluntly declared.

"Maybe you didn't. Maybe you did. That'll be for the jury over to Kingfish to decide. I'm sending a wire off to Sheriff Barton right after I get you locked up in the hoosegow." He wagged his rifle at Fargo's naked legs. "Why don't you do us both a favor and get your britches on? It's embarrassing the hell out of me to have you sitting there like that with a lady present."

Fargo slid to the end of the bed and started dressing. He noticed the deputies shift to cover him constantly. He also noticed one of the men holding his Sharps, Colt, and holster. "If it means anything,"he remarked, "I didn't know who was after me last night. I thought you were gunmen."

"Got a knack for making enemies, have you?" Marshal Howes said. "You're just damned lucky you didn't do more than wing one of my boys and bruise a few heads."

"Who'd I hit with the chair?"

"Me."

Fargo looked. There wasn't a bruise anywhere. "I thought I'd busted in your skull."

The lawman grinned and tapped his temple. "Not this noggin, mister. I've been hit by bottles, brooms, clubs, rocks, you name it, and never gotten a scratch. My grandpappy must have been part buffalo."

Straightening, Fargo shuffled to his boots, pretending to be so tired he could hardly think straight, when actually his mind was going like a thoroughbred at full gallop. He wanted them to think he was harmless so they'd lower their guard for the few moments it would take to get the drop on them.

Picking up his boots, Fargo stepped to the bed again. As he held the right boot close to his foot, he glanced inside without being obvious about it. The ankle sheath and Arkansas toothpick were both there, right where he had dropped them when he stripped last night. In the dark, Ellen hadn't seen his ace in

26

the hole.

"Hurry it up, Fargo," Marshal Howes ordered. "My missus is holding breakfast for me on account of you, and I don't want my two dozen eggs getting cold."

Fargo slid on the right boot, adjusting his foot so the hilt of the knife was under his arch and the slender sheath pointed forward. "Only two dozen?"

The huge lawman grinned. "I'm just getting over a cold, so my appetite isn't what it should be." He gestured at the door. "Now let's go. I promised not to shoot you outright, but I didn't say anything about not smacking you around a little if you got my goat."

"I'm on my way," Fargo said, tugging on the left boot. He donned his hat and walked toward the corridor, the deputies closing in around him. No matter which way he looked, a rifle muzzle stared him in the face.

Ellen preceded them. She was sniffling, and on reaching the lobby she stopped to dab her eyes. "I'm sorry, Skye," she said. "I know you're upset. I only hope you can find it in your heart to forgive me."

"You're forgiven," Fargo said. "Just don't expect me to recommend your hotel to any of my friends." A searing pang shot up his back as he was hit low down.

"What did I tell you about that smart mouth of yours?" the lawman said harshly. "In this town we treat ladies with respect."

Fargo should have known better, but his mouth seemed to reply of its own accord. "Your wife certainly has you well trained, Marshal. Do you jump through hoops for her, too?"

One of the deputies sucked in his breath. Another stepped back a stride. Then a steel hammer smashed Fargo squarely between the shoulder blades, the blow driving him to his knees. The lobby danced to a soundless jig, and his ears rang. A brawny hand seized him by the back of his shirt and hauled him off the floor. He was shoved so hard he stumbled through the front door and out into the dusty street. They expected him to sprawl in the dirt and lie there stunned, but he was tougher than any of them imagined. The instant his knees touched, he was up and running, speeding into the nearest alley.

Curses poured from the hotel ahead of the deputies and Marshal Howes. "Spread out!" the lawman thundered. "I want him found! And this time we don't go easy on the bastard!"

Dawn had broken not quiet half an hour ago. Fargo had no difficulty weaving among the piles of litter in the alley and out the other side. Going to the right would take him to the livery, which was where they'd count on him going, so he went left instead, sprinting past three structures before ducking into a recessed doorway as deputies spilled from the alley. He peeked, saw them heading toward the livery. Chuckling, he ran to the next alley and up it to the main street.

By now some of the good citizens of Ripclaw were abroad and being corralled by the marshal into lending a hand in the search. No one, as yet, had ventured near where Fargo stood.

Directly across the street stood the marshal's office. Fargo scoured the alley and saw a discarded basket. He also saw an old, shabby blanket. Folding the blanket in half, he threw it over his shoulder, wearing it like a serape. His hat went in the basket.

Marshal Howes and a goodly number of searchers were moving along the street toward the livery, their backs to Fargo. He hefted the basket to his shoulder, hiding his face, then boldly advanced toward the marshal's office, slouching to disguise his height.

No one called out. No one challenged him.

Fargo walked in as if he belonged there, then hastily discarded his disguise. He took a scattergun from a rack on the wall and rummaged in the desk for shells, which he found in the same drawer as a six-shooter, a Starr double-action .44.

Loading the shotgun took precedence. Then Fargo hefted the pistol, disliking both the feel and the balance. He had heard the new model revolvers were reliable and accurate, but he was too accustomed to his superb Colt to take much of a liking to the double-action. Still, it was the only pistol he could find, so he hastily loaded the cylinder and tucked the barrel under his belt.

In the street little had changed. The hunt was being concentrated in the vicinity of the livery.

Fargo went to the old stove, found it cold. He added wood

from the small pile and soon had flames crackling. Locating the coffee grounds was simple. In no time the delicious odor of percolating brew filled the room. He set two cups on the desk and held his hands to the stove to warm them. Suddenly, from the rear section, a man yelled.

"That you, you oversized son of a bitch?"

Drawing the Starr, Fargo stepped to the door separating the office from the jail. Beyond were two cells, only one of which was occupied, by a tall man with a scruffy beard and unkempt hair. Fargo opened the door and went in.

"Who the hell are you?" snapped the prisoner. "Where's the jackass who threw me in here?" He saw the pistol and re-coiled. "Now hold on, you! All I did was mouth off a little. That ain't no cause to be shooting somebody!"

Fargo halted at the bars. He got a whiff of the man and wished he hadn't. The prisoner apparently had yet to learn of the benefits of bathing. "What are you in for?" he asked.

"Hell if I know," the man snapped. "I got into town late yesterday and had a few drinks to celebrate. Next thing I know, a mountain wearing a badge drags me off and throws me in this rotten cell."

"Drunk and disorderly, I'd guess," Fargo said, turning to go. "Or maybe being a public nuisance. I hear it's against the law to deprive people of their right to breathe."

"What are you jabbering about?" the man demanded. "I haven't strangled no one." Coming to the bars, he sniffed loudly. "Is that Arbuckle's I smell? I'd take it kindly if you'd bring me a cup. My stomach is so empty it's inside out."

Fargo nodded and retraced his steps. A check of the street verified no one as yet was anywhere near the lawman's office. He filled a battered tin cup for the prisoner.

"Are you a deputy?" the man asked as Fargo passed the cup through a gap.

"No."

"Wondered why I didn't see a badge." Taking a loud sip, the prisoner smacked his lips, disclosing a set of rotten teeth. "What do you do? Help out by sweeping and emptying the chamber pots and such?"

"Not quite," Fargo answered, about to leave. He couldn't

stand to be in close proximity to the man for any length of time.

"I hope the marshal will let me out soon," the prisoner rambled on. "I have someplace to be in a few days." He took another sip. "First that barkeep gave me a hard time. Now this. Can't say much for the hospitality hereabouts."

"Don't expect a refill."

"Hold on. I didn't mean you, too," the man apologized. "You're decent enough." His thin hand slid through the bars. "Allow me to introduce myself. I'm Skye Fargo."

3

Very seldom was Skye Fargo taken so completely by surprise that he stood rooted with shock, speechless. He stared at the filthy prisoner in the cell and couldn't credit his own ears. This was the one impersonating him? And the man had been in the Ripclaw jail all along? He moved nearer, and something about his face caused the other Skye Fargo to jerk his hand in and back up.

"Hold on, mister. What's the matter with you? Why are you looking at me like you are?"

"What did you say your name was?" Fargo said. He had to hear it again to be sure.

The prisoner cocked his head, his flinty eyes narrowing. "Does that name mean something to you? Who are you, anyway?"

"I asked first." Fargo drew the Starr and aimed at the man's chest. "I need answers, and I need them now. Clam up on me and I'll put a bullet into each of your joints until you find your tongue."

"You can't do this!"

"Watch me," Fargo said, aiming at the man's right knee. Shots would bring the marshal and company on the run, so he was bluffing. But he was the only one who knew it, and from the stark fear contorting the prisoner's features, his bluff was having the desired effect. He was set to repeat his question when the clomp of boots on the boardwalk made him aware he had pushed his luck a bit too far.

Fargo dashed into the office and picked up the scattergun from the desk. He squatted behind the stove as the front door squeaked open.

"—care how long it takes," Marshal Howes was saying. "Round up every man in town who can carry a gun and go from door to door, room to room. Eventually we'll find him."

"Have a heart, Lee," another man protested. "That could take all day."

"So what? Would you rather a murderer got away? Do you want us to be the laughingstock of Texas when folks hear how we had him right in our grasp and let him escape?"

"All right. All right," the deputy grumbled. "I'll spread the word. But the boys aren't going to like having to keep on hunting while you take time off to eat breakfast."

"I can't help it. My stomach is rumbling so loud I can't hear myself think. Run along, Jasper, and do as I say."

The door closed, and Fargo rose high enough to see the lawman sink into the large chair at the desk. He leveled the scattergun over the top of the stove. Howes stretched, then gawked at the coffee cups, muttering, "What the hell! I didn't put them there." The lawman abruptly seemed to realize how warm the room was and glanced at the stove. "Fancy meeting you here," Fargo said.

Lee Howes froze. He was too seasoned a lawman to make a mad play for his hardware or to foolishly yell out. He did laugh, half to himself, and said, "Damned if you aren't the trickiest cuss I've ever come across, mister. I'm wearing out the soles of my boots searching all over Ripclaw for you, and the whole time you're in my own office, helping yourself to coffee."

Fargo came out from concealment. On a chair near the door were his pistol, rifle, and holster. Earlier he'd spotted his saddlebags and bedroll in a corner by the gun rack. All he needed to make his escape, except for the Ovaro. "Unbuckle your gun belt and fling it over by the stove," he directed.

Exaggerating his movements so Fargo would have no reason to shoot, the lawman did as he'd been told. Once unarmed, he sat back and clasped his huge hands behind his head. "You puzzle me, mister. You truly do. If you're the killer they claim, you would have blown me in half the moment I walked in the door."

"You're learning," Fargo said. Dragging the chair to the

corner, he pulled the Starr and propped the scattergun against the wall. In short order he had the Colt strapped around his waist and the loaded Sharps in hand. Every so often he'd gaze out the window. As yet, the only people he'd seen were a few women shopping at the general store and a farmer rattling up main street in a dilapidated wagon.

Fargo nodded at the jail. "What can you tell me about your prisoner?"

"Someone should dump him in a vat of lye and burn his clothes."

"Besides the obvious."

"There's not much else. I was about to head home last night when a local came in to let me know a stranger over at Wilson's saloon was acting up. So I went over, and sure enough there was this tall drink of water waving a pistol in the air and threatening to shoot anyone who moved." Howes sighed. "You know the type. A rip-snorting, whiskey-guzzling terror on two heels who can whip any man in the state with one arm tied behind his back."

"What did you do?"

"What I always do. I walked up to him real nice and polite, asking him sweet as you please to hand over his six-shooter. And when he blinked, I hit him so hard he landed on top of the bar. Then I dragged his carcass over here and threw him in a bunk."

"Did he tell you his name?"

"No. And I didn't ask. I was more concerned about getting that gun away from him before he shot somebody."

Fargo nodded toward the rear. "Then it's time you were properly introduced. You go first, and don't stop until you're in front of his cell."

The prisoner eyed them suspiciously. He was seated on the bunk, picking at his teeth with a sliver of wood. "Howdy there, Marshal," he addressed Howes. "I can't say as I think very highly of the help you hire. That hombre behind you was fixing to put holes in me before you came back."

"Was he now?" The lawman swiveled. "What is this all about?"

Pointing at the man in the cell, Fargo said, "Tell him your name."

"Why should I?"

"Because you like to breathe."

Standing, the prisoner threw the sliver at his feet in disgust. "I don't have the foggiest notion what is going on here, but I never talk back to someone who is loco." He grinned at the marshal. "My handle is Wes Tucker."

Fargo took a step nearer. "Tell him the name you told me."

"I don't know what you're talking about. My name is Wes Tucker and it's always been Wes Tucker. What do you take me for?"

It suddenly dawned on Fargo that the prisoner might be a lot smarter than he appeared. Fargo tried his bluff again, sighting down the Sharps at Tucker's head. "I want the truth."

"All right. I'm President James Buchanan. Or maybe you'd be happier if I was Jim Bowie?" Tucker snapped his fingers. "No, I can't hardly be him. Bowie died at the Alamo."

Marshal Howes leaned on the bars and folded his arms. "What are you getting at?" he asked Fargo. "I don't much care who this idiot is. Soon as I can, I'm sending him packing. And if he ever shows his face in Ripclaw again, I'll rip it off."

"You should care. He told me his name is Skye Fargo."

The lawman glanced at Tucker, then burst into hearty laughter. "You're slipping, mister, if you think I'm dumb enough to fall for a stunt this stupid. Pinning the blame on Tucker is a waste of my time and yours."

To Fargo's annoyance, the man now calling himself Wes Tucker joined in the mirth. Fargo stepped even closer, longing to get his hands on the conniving coyote. For a thoughtless moment he took his eyes off the marshal, but that moment was all it took.

Uncoiling with startling speed for one so huge, Marshal Lee Howes sprang. He caught Fargo around the upper chest, his enormous arms clamping as tight as a vise. Fargo tried to twist, to swing the Sharps into the lawman's stomach, but Howes swept him off the floor before he could and slammed him into the bars. Stars exploded in front of Fargo and he dropped the rifle. Dazed, he sagged. The lawman slackened his grip a little and said, "I reckon that'll teach you to buck me, mister."

The marshal was wrong. Fargo let Howes start to lower him to the floor, then he set his feet flat and whipped both arms upward. The heels of his palms caught the underside of the lawman's chin and snapped Howes's head back with a loud crack. The marshal staggered rearward, into the wall, and had to brace himself to stay upright.

Fargo waded in, fists flying. He landed a right to the stomach that folded Howes in half, then a left to the head that would have knocked out most men. Howes rolled with the blow and delivered a backhand. Fargo ducked, jabbed three punches in swift succession to the midsection. It was like striking a tree. Howes was as muscular as he was big.

The marshal drove his knee into Fargo's chest, hurling Fargo against the cell. Fargo sidestepped a kick, feinted with his left, and followed through with a right that rocked the larger man on his heels.

Howes glided a few feet away, shaking his head vigorously. Raising his fists like a boxer, he commented, "You're tough. I'll give you that. But there isn't a man alive who can go toe to toe with me."

Fargo had two choices. He could fight the marshal on the lawman's own terms or he could resort to the Colt. Given Howes's character, Fargo knew he'd have to shoot Howes to stop him, and Fargo didn't care to have the marshal's blood on his hands. So he brought both fists up and moved to meet the lawman halfway.

It soon became apparent that Lee Howes relied more on strength than skill. Howes punched steadily, mechanically, straight out from the shoulder or in brutal uppercuts. Fargo, on the other hand, was adept at those tactics but also good at jabs, hooks, and crosses. Fargo was also faster, more agile. So they were more evenly matched than seemed apparent.

Lee Howes struck first, or tried to, each and every one of his punches missing. Fargo retaliated with a right to the cheek, a left to the ribs, and another right, this time to the jaw. The marshal, scowling, aimed an uppercut that Fargo neatly avoided.

As the fight went on, Fargo became more confident. He'd rarely gone up against anyone as big as the lawman, but he held his own with ease. And when, after blocking a blow that stung both forearms, he buried a fist in the marshal's side and heard Howes grunt in pain and pant, he knew it was only a matter of time before he wore the other man down—provided nothing unforeseen occurred. But it did.

Constantly shifting one way or the other, turning as needed to evade a punch or strike, Fargo lost track of exactly where he stood in relation to the office and the cells. He had no idea he was close to Tucker's cell until Howes clipped him on the collarbone, tumbling him against the cell door. As he straightened, a pair of dirty hands encircled him from behind, pinning him in place.

"I got him for you, Marshal!" Wes Tucker barked. "Hit him a good one for me!"

Lee Howes was bleeding in several places, the worst a cut over his right eye. He swiped at the blood as he set himself and formed his right hand into a massive mallet. "You've done better than anyone else, ever," he said through puffy lips. "Didn't figure you had it in you." Drawing back his arm, he steadied himself. "Now it ends."

Fargo saw the lawman's bulging neck muscles ripple as the arm streaked at his face. Desperately he dropped, tearing his left arm loose and diving to one side. There was a loud clang and Howes roared in torment. Fargo glanced up, saw the marshal clutching his arm and blood pouring from several crackled knuckles. He snatched Tucker's wrist, then heaved forward, yanking the prisoner into the bars. Tucker's forehead thudded hard and he sagged, letting go.

Gaining his feet, Fargo pounded a right into Howes, just under the left eye. Howes tottered but stayed erect. Fargo clasped his hands together, then swung them as he might a club. The marshal flew backwards, the rear of his head smashing into the bars. Howes sagged, swayed, and fell onto his knees.

"Stay down," Fargo said.

Lee Howes had no intention of listening. Veins bulging, he regained his footing and faced Fargo. All the spark was gone, the fire in his eyes mere embers. He was a shell of his former self as he staggered forward, game to the last.

"Some men never learn," Fargo remarked, but not as an insult. Any man who hung true to his convictions and kept on fighting even when beaten was a man worthy of respect. Fargo planted his boots, and when Howes attempted an awkward swing that missed, he executed a perfect punch that didn't.

The marshal keeled over like a giant tree in the forest, the impact of his body shaking the entire floor. Fargo lifted the lawman's head, verifying Howes was unconscious. Once assured, he retrieved the Sharps and turned.

"Don't you hurt me!" Wes Tucker rasped, scampering into a back corner. "I was only doing my duty by helping that lawdog!"

"I want some answers," Fargo said.

"Go to hell! It's plain you ain't no lawman. Nor hired help. You won't get diddly out of me, stranger. Not now, not ever."

"We'll see about that." Fargo went into the office and found a large key ring hanging from a short peg. The first key didn't work so he inserted the next. The tumblers worked smoothly and he swung the door outward.

Tucker cowered, his hands raised to protect his face. "Don't you lay a finger on me! If you do, I swear my kin will hunt you down and make you regret the day you were born! They're rattler-mean, my brothers. And they've killed more men than you can shake a stick at."

"Sure they have," Fargo said, leveling the Sharps. He recognized an inveterate liar when he saw one. "Let's go."

"I'm not going anywhere with you!"

Fargo could ill afford to delay. Striding up to Tucker, he grabbed the man's wrist and flung him the length of the room. Tucker lost his balance, tripped over his own feet, and hit the bars headfirst. Stunned, he slumped on his hands and knees.

Going over, Fargo gripped the back of Tucker's shirt, then gave the prisoner a boost through the doorway with the toe of his boot. Tucker whined and scrambled up.

"Please, mister! I can't stand pain! Lay off me and I'll see that you get all the money you can carry! Coins, too. Gold, if you want. Or silver."

"Keep your mouth shut until I say otherwise," Fargo directed, taking Tucker's arm and propelling him into the office. He shoved Tucker into the chair behind the desk. "If you move, I'll shoot your foot off."

"My foot?"

"You don't need toes to talk," Fargo pointed out. Opening the drawers, he soon located an extra badge, which he pinned on his buckskin shirt. He watched Tucker out of the corner of one eye and stepped to the front window.

The search was in full swing, with dozens of citizens taking part. Some women had joined in as a lark and were chatting and laughing as they went from building to building. To Fargo's amazement, even kids were being permitted to participate and were dashing around with toy guns in hand. "A regular family affair," he said.

"What are you fixing to do?" Wes Tucker asked. "There's no way you can escape from Ripclaw, now if all them folks are after you."

"I told you to shut up," Fargo reminded the man, wagging the Sharps.

Tucker tried to melt into the chair, pleading, "Lord, be careful with that cannon! I seen a man shot with one once. Put a hole in him the size of a cantaloupe."

"And they have hair triggers," Fargo mentioned, which closed Tucker's mouth with a snap. "Remember that if you get any ideas."

Fargo edged to the door, studying the faces of the men nearest the marshal's office. None were deputies from the hotel, as near as he could determine, and no one else had gotten a good look at him except for Ellen and the liveryman. Most were townspeople conscripted into the hunt. Opening the door, he stood in the doorway and motioned at a likely candidate, a portly man in a derby who was several buildings down. "Marshal Howes has something he'd like you to do, friend."

The man hurried up. "What now? It's bad enough I had to close shop to go on this silly wild-goose chase. I'm a merchant, damn it, not a gunfighter."

"Relax, friend," Fargo said amiably. "All you have to do is

go to the livery and tell Eli you want Fargo's Ovaro and the horse that belongs to the drunk. Make sure Eli saddles them."

"What in the world does Lee want the horses for?"

"I don't know and I'm not about to ask. He's not in the best of moods. But you're welcome to ask him yourself." Fargo made as if to move aside.

"Never mind," the merchant said. "I know how he can get, and I don't want him jumping down my throat. I'll fetch the horses. But I don't have to like it." He walked off in a huff.

Fargo slipped inside, closed the door. Wes Tucker had done something smart for once and not moved. "When the horses get here, you'll mount up without talking to anyone. Head south. I'll be beside you the whole time."

"Who *are* you?"

"All in good time," Fargo said, preferring to keep his identity secret until he learned the truth about Tucker. He'd never met the man before, and it was clear Tucker had never so much as seen him, or Tucker would have known who he was the moment they met. Why, then, had Tucker impersonated him? Why have blame for the four deaths put on his shoulders? What was the filthy man hoping to gain? There were so many questions.

Fargo indicated his saddlebags and bedroll. "Pick them up and bring them along."

Like a dog cringing in fear of its master's lash, Tucker scooted to do Fargo's bidding. He sat down in the chair with the articles in his lap. "I bet you're an outlaw," he commented thoughtfully. "That's what this is all about, isn't it? You're a wanted man. But I don't recollect seeing any circulars on you."

Ignoring him, Fargo watched the stable. He saw the merchant go in. The minutes went by with unnerving slowness. More searchers were in the area of the jail. Several deputies appeared, instructing their helpers, and Fargo ducked back until the deputies entered a high frame structure.

Presently, the merchant reappeared leading the two horses. Eli was with them. They took their sweet time bringing the animals, stopping twice to talk.

Fargo gestured and Tucker came to within a yard of the

door. "Don't so much as blink," Fargo said, moving behind him and bending at the knees. This close, the smell was enough to gag a polecat.

Eli and the merchant paused at the hitching post to tie the horses. The merchant shook his head at something the livery-man said, then walked off. Shrugging, Eli stepped onto the boardwalk and opened the door, halting in surprise on encountering Wes Tucker. "Who are you? Where's Howes? I have a bone to pick with him about the reward."

Popping up, Fargo fixed a bead on Eli's gaping mouth. "At this range I can't miss. One word out of you and I'll prove it." He stepped to the right. "Away from the door. Now!"

The flabbergasted liveryman complied without complaint, automatically raising his arms. "I figured it was strange for Lee to want your pinto so soon," he said. "He told me that he wouldn't be taking you to Kingfish for a day or two."

"What was that about a reward?" Fargo asked.

"The daughter of the boardinghouse owners you killed put a five-hundred-dollar bounty on your head, but you have to be delivered alive for anyone to collect."

Now there was a new one, Fargo mused. By all rights the daughter should want him dead. "Were Lee and you going to split the money?"

"Hell, no," Eli said. "Lee doesn't want no part of the bounty, which suits me fine. Since I was the one who turned you in to the law, I should be the one who collects."

"Thanks for reminding me," Fargo said politely, and slugged the liveryman. Eli buckled, groaning as he hit the floor. Stepping over him, Fargo checked the street in both directions. A few women and children were near the hitching post, and approaching from the general store was an elderly man on horseback. Far down near a saloon stood one of the deputies, but he was busy charming a young woman.

Fargo prodded Tucker with the Sharps. "Walk straight to my horse and tie on the bedroll and saddlebags. Then, and only then, climb on your sorrel. Savvy?"

"Don't worry, mister. After what I've seen of you, I'm not about to invite an early grave. And now that I've had some time to think about it, I'm as eager to quit this town as you are." Tucker brazenly walked out. He smiled at the women, which offended their dignity so much they rushed off, shooing the kids ahead of them. "Don't know what it is," he said, cackling. "I always have that effect."

"Move it," Fargo snapped, strolling to the stallion with his head bowed low. He anxiously scanned Ripclaw as Tucker secured his belongings. When Tucker turned to the sorrel, he loosened the Ovaro's reins, stepped into the stirrups, and slid the Sharps into its scabbard.

At that moment, out of a nearby store walked two of the men who had helped Marshal Howes arrest him. The shorter of the pair glanced at Fargo, glanced away, then jumped as if he'd stepped on a cactus. Clawing for his six-shooter, he screamed loud enough to be heard from one end of town to the other, "It's him! Fargo! The killer! He's escaping!"

"Ride!" Fargo told Tucker, and took the lead, wheeling sharply and making a beeline toward open country as all around them guns opened up.

4

Few of Ripclaw's citizens were sharpshooters, and their marksmanship was made worse by the seething confusion that resulted in the first few moments after the deputy squawked in alarm. Skye Fargo bent low over his stallion, lashing with the reins. Bullets whizzed overhead. Somewhere glass shattered. He galloped past a man too befuddled to unlimber a pistol. A woman ran screaming hysterically from his path. Then a townsman carrying a rifle sped from a building on the left and took aim.

Fargo veered, his spurs pricking the pinto's flanks. The Ovaro slammed into the rifleman as the rifle went off, discharging harmlessly into the ground. The man flew into the corner of the building and collapsed.

More shots boomed as Fargo passed the last house. He promptly cut to the left, putting the house between the shooters and himself. A look back showed Wes Tucker on the stallion's heels. Together they galloped to the nearest hill. On the crest, Fargo glanced around again and discovered a small posse in swift pursuit.

"Stick with me!" Wes Tucker shouted. "I know this country better than they do!" His legs pounding the sides of his sorrel, he angled down the slope to the southwest.

Fargo was not about to let the impersonator out of his sight. He stayed on the sorrel's tail as they wound through a strip of woodland, crossed a meadow being grazed by cattle, and clattered up the rocky slope of another hill. The posse was just cresting the first one. Someone rashly snapped off a rifle shot, even though the distance was much too great.

Wes Tucker demonstrated he was, in this instance, as good

as his word. He picked a circuitous route through the densest of brush and over the driest, hardest of ground, a route intended to leave few prints and give their pursuers no end of grief.

The man's skill was so exceptional, Fargo was impressed. He suspected Tucker must be well accustomed to being on the run. They covered a mile without drawing another shot, and by then they had a substantial lead.

By midday the posse was no longer in sight. Tucker slowed, his sorrel hanging its head. "We need to give the horses a breather." His eyes shifted to the stallion. "My horse, anyhow. Yours could go another twenty miles and not work up a sweat."

Fargo rested a hand on his leg, within quick reach of the Colt. "Start bearing due south."

"What for?"

"We're heading for Kingfish."

Tucker yanked on his reins, stopping. "Like hell we are. I'm not setting foot in that town again for all the gold in the Rockies."

"You're a little mixed up."

"How so?"

"You think you have a choice."

"Damn it all!" Tucker blew steam. "I've had enough of you pushing me around like I was a measly tenderfoot! I'm a dangerous man. My kin will skin you alive if you keep prodding me."

"So you keep saying." Fargo patted his pistol. "But these kin of yours are nowhere around, and I have five reasons here why you had better loosen your tongue. I want to know why you claimed to be Skye Fargo."

"How do you know I ain't?"

Fargo was about to reveal his identity in the belief it might so shock Tucker the man would spill all he knew. Then it occurred to him that it could have the opposite impact than the one he wanted. Tucker might seal his lips and not talk no matter what was done to him. So, acting on inspiration, he responded, "I happen to know the real Skye Fargo."

"You do?" Tucker declared. "Are you a friend of his?"

"Not exactly."

"Then why were you so fired up about learning the truth? You acted like him and you were best pards."

Thinking fast, Fargo said, "I happen to know he's in this area. He'd be interested to hear of someone impersonating him. So interested he'd be willing to pay for the information."

Tucker brightened. "So that's your angle! Why, you sneaky son of a bitch! You're hauling me off to Kingfish to turn me over to him, aren't you? Then you'll ride off with a full poke and he'll carve me into teensy pieces."

"Something like that," Fargo said, bracing for the angry outburst sure to follow. To his surprise, Tucker cackled crazily and slapped his leg.

"Don't this beat everything I've ever heard! You're a man after my own heart, mister. Why, I'd turn in my own ma if there was money to be made." Tucker scratched under one arm. "But I've got some news for you. If you go asking around for Skye Fargo in Kingfish, you're liable to be strung up so fast it'll make your head swim."

"Why?" Fargo shammed ignorance.

"Because Fargo is wanted for killing four people, that's why." Tucker tittered. "I know for a fact, because I passed through Kingfish about the same time he did."

A glaring flaw in the filthy man's account made Fargo ask, "If that's the case, why did you claim to be him the first time we talked?"

"Sheer dumbness," Tucker said, sniffing the tips of his fingers. "I wasn't fully awake yet and was half hungover from my celebration the night before. So I up and said the first name that popped into my head." He winked slyly. "I couldn't very well give my real name, not when there's a sheriff or two who would be delighted to hear of my whereabouts."

Fargo was disappointed. Tucker's explanation made sense, especially since Tucker was more than a few cards shy of a full deck. His fervent hope of gleaning facts about the slayings were dashed.

"No, sir," the man gabbed on. "You'd be smart to steer clear of Kingfish. They're in a lynching mood in that town. Any stranger looks at them crosswise will live to regret it."

The prediction had a ring of truth to it. Fargo would be playing with fire if he went there to uncover the truth. Yet, what else was there to do? he asked himself. Once word spread, every lawman west of the Mississippi River would be on the lookout for him. He'd be a marked man, always on the run, never knowing when the crack of a gun would be the last sound he heard. Fargo had to clear his name. It was that simple. And there was only one way to do it.

"So what is it to be?" Tucker continued. "Do you drag me off to Kingfish and likely get us both killed, or will you let me go about my own business and you go about yours?"

"You're free to ride anywhere you please," Fargo said reluctantly.

"Praise the Lord! He's seen the light!" Tucker exclaimed, then laughed some more. "Since you're being so reasonable, I won't hold our tussle in the jail against you. Now how about doing me another favor and letting me have that Starr?"

Fargo had forgotten about the double-action, which he had tucked under his belt after strapping on the Colt. He pulled it out, but hesitated.

"You can't let me go off unarmed," Tucker urged. "This is Comanche country, not to mention all the thieves and cutthroats who prey on lone riders. I won't make it to Sawtooth without something to protect myself."

Against his better judgment, Fargo handed the Starr over—after removing the cartridges and dumping them on the ground. "You can pick them up after I'm gone," he said. By the time Tucker reloaded, he'd be out of pistol range.

"I'm obliged," Tucker said, hefting the revolver. "If you ever get to south Texas, to the Staked Plain country, you look me up. Everyone there knows me, so I won't be hard to find. We'll share a few drinks and talk about old times." Cackling once more, he deftly twirled the Starr.

Fargo rode southward without another word. He'd stomached all of Tucker he could. It was nice to be able to breathe normally again, and he took deep breaths to clear his lungs. He looked back twice to confirm the strange man wasn't reloading. Soon he entered a patch of trees. He couldn't say what prompted him to rein up and look around the trunk of the oak he'd just passed, but he did, and there was Tucker scrambling over the ground to find the bullets as if his life depended on replacing them in the next few seconds.

Shaking his head at the man's antics, Fargo pressed on. Hills continued to break the surface of the rolling prairie. The lush grass fed deer, antelope, and small knots of buffalo that were part of a larger herd that roamed as far south as the Rio Grande.

Fargo was in his element. He was more at home in the wilderness than he was in towns and cities, which had their charms but could not begin to compete with a clear azure sky, rippling grassland, and the panorama of wildlife. In the wild a man could forget his cares, could relax and take each day as it came along without having to worry about being shot in the back by a weasel like Wes Tucker.

It had taken Fargo two days of hard riding to reach Ripclaw from Kingfish. He took his time on the return trip, staying away from the established trail to avoid trouble. At times the trail came into sight off to the left, and during one of those times he spied a large knot of men riding hell-for-leather toward Kingfish. His first thought was that it was a posse, after him, but on reflection he realized that Howes had no way of knowing he would head for Kingfish, so it couldn't be.

Evening of the third day brought the lights of the town into sight. Fargo circled Kingfish once, seeking the best way to approach. A dry wash lined with brush brought him to the outskirts. He tied the Ovaro to a bush, removed his spurs and stuffed them in his saddlebags, then quietly stalked to within a stone's throw of a side street.

Kingfish was slightly bigger than Ripclaw, with a half-dozen more saloons, two churches instead of one, and a hotel twice the size of Eleanor Seaver's. Kingfish being the county seat, the residents spared themselves the expense of hiring a marshal by relying on the sheriff, Neal Barton, a tough customer by all accounts.

Fargo crept to the side street, careful to stay in the shadows. An alley took him to the main street, which bustled with activity. A few women were doing last-minute shopping before hurrying home to fix late suppers. Farmers and ranchers were arriving to hoist a few drinks and hear the latest tidings. Townsmen strolled about, enjoying the cool air after the heat of the day.

Of special interest to Fargo was the sheriff's office, from which a lantern gleamed, and the bulletin board outside it where the lawman tacked wanted posters and town regulations. Was a circular on him hanging there? he wondered. He had to know if the sheriff had a good description, and whether he could safely mingle in Kingfish.

Pulling his hat brim low, Fargo hooked his thumbs in his gun belt and sauntered across the street. No one regarded him with more than idle interest. The bulletin board contained five posters, all bearing ink sketches of the outlaws wanted, but none referred to him. Someone, though, had put up the first page of the *Kingfish Courier*, bearing the banner headline: MURDERS MOST FOUL. He read about the discovery of the victims, how the daughter of the boardinghouse owners had stumbled upon them when she returned from a church social. The father had still been alive, lingering long enough to tell the daughter the name of the man responsible and supply a description.

Suddenly the door to the sheriff's office opened. Fargo turned, pretending to scratch his chin to hide the lower half of his face. Footsteps moved away from him, and when he risked a glance he saw a lean man wearing a black broadcloth coat walking off.

Fargo strolled in the opposite direction, mulling over his options. He had about made up his mind to seek out the daughter and question her, when he came abreast of a saloon. It was the same saloon where he had met the faro dealer who told him about one of the Jeffers brothers passing through.

Fargo peered over the batwing doors at the gambling section of the room. A poker game was underway, but as yet the faro table was empty. He heard someone coming up behind him and turned to get out of the way. And nearly bumped into the faro dealer himself.

The man had been fiddling with his watch chain. He looked up, started to say, "Didn't see——" and stopped, startled. Eyes widening, he exclaimed, "You!"

"Me," Fargo said.

"You've got your nerve." The man glanced up and down the street. "You're a wanted man, in case you haven't heard. The law is looking all over for you."

"I know. We need to talk."

"Sure, mister," the dealer said, swallowing. "Come to my table while I set up."

"No. A private talk," Fargo stressed. It would be folly to venture inside when the sheriff might unexpectedly show up at any time, making his rounds. "Somewhere we won't be disturbed."

"The alley," the dealer suggested, bearing right into a gloomy passageway between the saloon and a mercantile. He walked past piles of refuse, past a door in the side of the saloon, to the far back, where a rickety fence barred them from going farther. "Will this do?"

"It's fine," Fargo said, twisting to see if anyone had noticed them. Almost too late, he caught the glint of metal out of the corner of his eye. He brought his hands up as a dagger snaked at his throat. Catching hold of the dealer's wrist, he heaved, throwing the dealer off balance. The man snarled and kicked, hitting Fargo in the shin. The dealer's other hand closed on Fargo's throat and squeezed.

It all happened so fast that Fargo was taken aback. The dealer had been friendly when last they met; Fargo had no reason to suspect treachery. At the time, Fargo had been going from saloon to saloon, asking all the faro dealers if anyone answering Bob Jeffers's description had played recently. The younger Jeffers was addicted to the game. It was rumored he couldn't pass up a faro table without trying his luck. So naturally Fargo had checked around.

Now, as the sallow-faced dealer grunted and strained to bury his dagger in Fargo's neck, Fargo knew he had been duped. But for the life of him he couldn't imagine why. The dealer didn't know him. Why had the man lied? Why send him on to Ripclaw, knowing full well Jeffers wasn't there?

The man was growing frantic. Fargo slowly forced the knife backwards, his superior strength prevailing. Hissing in rage, the dealer lashed out with a leg, hooking it behind Fargo's left foot while simultaneously shoving. Fargo fell, but he pulled the dealer along with him, jabbing a foot into the man's stomach and rolling as he went down. Flinging his leg outward, Fargo catapulated the dealer into the mercantile wall.

Growling in baffled fury, the man stood. He bent at the waist, the dagger held in front of him in the classic knife-fighter's stance. "I don't know how you figured it out," he said, "but I'm not letting you live to tell the sheriff."

Fargo had no idea what the man was talking about. Skipping rearward to avoid a slash, he quickly stopped, sliding a hand inside his right boot to grab the Arkansas toothpick, which rested snug in its ankle sheath. The toothpick streaked clear. Fargo lunged, but the faro dealer pranced out of reach. Keen blades flicking at one another like the long fangs of snakes, they circled, each seeking a gap in the other's guard.

A man and a woman went by the alley entrance, the woman laughing loudly. The faro dealer froze until they passed, showing he dreaded discovery as much as Fargo.

"Why?" Fargo asked in the all-too-brief respite. "Why did you lie?"

"Why else?" the dealer rejoined. "Money." With that he attacked, trying to slip his dagger past the toothpick, to end the fight immediately.

Fargo's shoulders brushed against the wall of the saloon. He feinted, parried a thrust, and stabbed. The toothpick bit into the dealer's chest, but not deeply, not fatally, and the dealer, incensed, redoubled his efforts.

Gamblers were notorious for their proficiency with knives and derringers. This one was a credit to his profession. He tried every trick ever invented to slip Fargo's defenses and draw blood, but was denied time and again. Then he showed that his skill was not as polished as it should be. Growing impatient, he overextended himself while driving the dagger down low.

Fargo had only to pivot and stab. The toothpick penetrated the dealer's rib cage and the man rose on his toes, face blank with astonishment. Fargo wrenched, shearing through flesh, then jerked his arm back.

The dealer turned to mush, sinking to his knees, wheezing

through his nose. "You've killed me, damn you," he said feebly. "Never thought it would be like this."

Wary of getting too close, Fargo said, "You mentioned money. Did someone pay you to send me on to Ripclaw?"

A bitter laugh rattled in the man's throat. Blood bubbled from his mouth. "What a stupid way to go! And all for two hundred dollars."

"Who paid you?" Fargo asked, sliding a little nearer. "Who wanted me out of the way, and why?"

"You don't understand anything," the dealer said, looking up in stony resentment. "They're playing you for a jackass, mister. Before they're done, you'll be sorry you ever set foot in Texas."

"Who are you talking about? Frank and Bob Jeffers?" In his eagerness to learn more, Fargo sidled even closer, the dripping toothpick at his side.

"Go to hell!" the dealer said. "I was raised in the same town they were. We were pards long before they took to the owl-hoot trail." A coughing spasm hit him and he doubled over, retching. When it subsided, he lifted his head and sneered. "I'll get some satisfaction out of going to my grave knowing I didn't turn them in." He laughed hollowly. "They've done you good, they have!"

"I need to know more!" Fargo insisted, taking one more step.

The dealer abruptly unwound like a coiled spring, driving the dagger at Fargo's heart. He'd deliberately lured Fargo nearer in the hope of taking Fargo with him.

Fargo had suspected as much, so he was ready. As the man moved, so did he, twisting aside and grasping the man's arm. He rammed his knee into the dealer's elbow, heard a loud crack. The dealer cried out, his dagger falling.

"I need to know!" Fargo demanded, leaning over. The dealer smiled at him, lips moving weakly. A single word came out, a word that made no sense whatsoever.

"*Ooth.*"

"What?" Fargo asked. Fate deprived him of an answer, for the next moment the dealer exhaled long and loud, then drooped, lifeless.

Thwarted, Fargo let the man slump to the earth and straighten. He knew little more than he had before, but enough to know someone was playing him for a fool. The Jefferses were the likeliest suspects, although how they had learned he was after them was hard to imagine. He squatted to wipe the toothpick on the dealer's gray jacket, then replaced the knife in its sheath.

The door in the side of the saloon opened, and Fargo flattened. He saw a stocky bartender emerge holding an empty whiskey crate, which the man set against the wall. The bartender turned to go back in, then paused, staring at the end of the alley.

"Hey! What's going on there?"

Fargo rose on one knee and slurred his voice to give the impression he'd had ten drinks too many. "Keep the noise down, will you? Can't you see we're trying to sleep?"

"Damn idiots," the bartender said, advancing. "How many times have I told you to sleep it off in your rooms?" He slowed, staring at the dealer. "Say. Wait a minute. Isn't that Mitchem? What's he doing drunk when he's supposed to be working a table tonight? The boss will have his head for this."

"And yours, too," Fargo guessed, sweeping upward with his fist lashing in a tight arc. The bartender was tough. He staggered with the first blow, then attempted to bring his arms up. Fargo slugged him again and the man spun slowly onto a pile of trash.

Rushing to the door, Fargo listened a moment to rowdy conversation, guffaws, and the tinkle of a poorly played piano. He shut the door and hastened to the street, making sure no one was nearby before turning left and heading toward the side street that would take him to the wash and the pinto. He had to get out of town before the bartender was found.

Several men lounged in front of the sheriff's office, including the one in the black broadcloth coat.

Sheriff Barton, Fargo figured, and decided to cross the street a block sooner. He timed it so he crossed at the same time a small group of boisterous cowboys came from the other side. Once on the boardwalk, he glanced at the sheriff and was disturbed to see Barton staring in his direction.

Fargo acted as if he didn't have a care in the world, stopping to gaze at the merchandise in the window of the general store. In the reflection he could see the lawman, who started to cross the street with the others.

Resisting an impulse to run, Fargo strode to the next building, looking for a doorway he could duck into. The sign painted on the front of the building caught his eye. KNOBEL BOARDING-HOUSE. It was the boardinghouse where the murders had taken place! Through the window he glimpsed a woman working at a counter—perhaps the daughter herself, the one who claimed he was to blame.

Fargo shifted his eyes to the left. Sheriff Barton and the other two men were now on the same side of the street, walking slowly toward him. They didn't act as if they suspected his identity, but Fargo wasn't taking any chances. Squaring his shoulders, he faced the door, turned the knob, and entered the boardinghouse.

5

The young woman swung around. "Looking for a room?" she inquired politely.

Skye Fargo stopped, thunderstruck. He had met more than his share of lovely women in his time, yet few could hold a candle to the raven-haired beauty regarding him with a mixture of curiosity and earthy interest. She had striking green eyes, high cheekbones, and lips like strawberries, and her dress clung to her body as if sculpted by a master sculptor.

"Sir?" she coaxed when he said nothing.

"Yes, I am," Fargo fibbed. "How much do you charge a night?"

"Fifty cents. A dollar if you take breakfast." She bestowed a dazzling smile on him that belied an underlying air of deep sadness. "And I bet a big, strapping specimen like yourself eats a hearty breakfast."

"Sometimes," Fargo allowed. He walked to the counter as the sheriff's party appeared outside. They neither slowed nor looked in. Relaxing, he leaned on the counter, disliking what he must do next.

"Tomorrow there will be fresh eggs from Potter's farm, and all the flapjacks you can eat," the woman said. "We pride ourselves at Knobel Boardinghouse on providing the very best for those who stay with us."

"Knobel Boardinghouse?" Fargo repeated. "Didn't I just read about your place over on the bulletin board?"

The sadness intensified. The woman lowered her head and shook ever so slightly. "Yes, you did," she said softly. "I'm Lorraine Knobel. Those were my folks who were killed."

"Have they caught the one who did it? What was his name again? Fargo?"

"Skye Fargo." Lorraine looked up, new vigor animating her features, the vigor of sheer and total hatred. "No, they haven't apprehended him yet, but Sheriff Barton assures me it's only a matter of time." She gazed at a framed photograph of an elderly couple and her eyes moistened. "They arrested him in Ripclaw, but he got away. The man has more lives than a cat."

"Ripclaw, you say?" Fargo went on with his act. "I'm heading that way myself. Sure hope I don't run into this hardcase. Does anyone know what he looks like?"

"I thought I did," Lorraine said uncertainly.

"Ma'am?"

"Oh, it's nothing," she said, brushing at her hair. "Just a little misunderstanding. You see, I found my father alive, and he gave me a description of the man who knifed him. But later the sheriff was given a completely different description by someone else in town."

"Which one is the right one?" Fargo pressed her despite his misgivings. The newspaper hadn't mentioned that someone else volunteered information, and he was eager to discover who and track the person down.

"If you don't mind," Lorraine Knobel said huskily, "I'd rather not discuss it. The subject is much too painful."

"Of course. I'm sorry for bothering you." Fargo touched his hat and went to leave.

"Wait. What about that room?"

"I've changed my mind. Thanks." Fargo looked to the left as he exited. The sheriff had disappeared into one of the buildings, so the coast was clear for him to hurry to the side street and from there to the wash. He mounted, then walked the stallion along the bottom of the wash for half a mile.

For Fargo to remain in the vicinity of Kingfish was foolhardy. Yet he didn't see where he had any recourse. In order to find the man impersonating him, he had to unravel a lot more details than he already knew.

A stand of trees provided a safe haven until dawn. Fargo made a cold camp. Bundled in his blankets, he stayed awake until late, reviewing everything that had happened. He thought of sending a wire to Arthur Walker, the man who had hired him, yet he didn't see what good it would do. Walker would vouch for his integrity, but he would still need to turn himself in to the law. And that he wouldn't do until he got to the heart of the mystery.

It was the rattle of a buckboard that awakened Fargo shortly after sunrise. He sat up and ran a hand through his hair, thinking he had accidentally made camp near a road. To his dismay, there was a road, a hundred yards distant. Much closer lay a cemetery, the graves forming irregular rows extending to within a few dozen feet of the trees. He quickly slid out from under his blankets and rolled his bedroll.

The wagon had turned into the graveyard and stopped. A lone figure climbed down, then made her way toward the rear of the graveyard. She carried two roses in her gloved hands. A narrow-rimmed black hat shaded the upper half of her face, preventing Fargo from seeing her eyes until she stopped beside a freshly dug grave and respectfully removed it. Kneeling, she reverently placed the roses on the pile of dirt.

Fargo had the Ovaro saddled by then. Leaving the pinto there, he walked into the open. His spurs were still in his saddlebags, so she didn't hear him until he was almost upon her, then she spun and stood.

"You again!" Lorraine Knobel declared.

"Me again."

"What are you doing here? Were you following me?"

"No," Fargo said. "But we do need to talk and this is as good a place as any. Here we won't be disturbed."

"Look, mister, I don't know you. And after what happened to my parents, I'm not letting you come anywhere near me. So if you'll be so kind, move aside."

"I can't."

Lorraine clearly did not know whether to scream, bolt, or fight. She fingered her hat and glanced at the buckboard.

"You'd never beat me to it," Fargo said.

"What do you want?"

"I'm not going to hurt you, if that's what is bothering you," Fargo assured her, making no uncalled-for movements. "I

55

want to hear about your parents from your own lips, then I'll be on my way."

"Why are you so interested? They didn't know you, or I'd know you. What's your interest in their deaths?"

"I'd rather not say," Fargo said, taking a few more steps so he was close enough to tackle her if she made a run for it. "Please. Just humor me and I'll be out of your hair."

The daughter made no effort to hide her confusion. "Since I have no choice, I'll take you at your word. But I won't go into detail. And then I want you to go, immediately." She took a breath to steady herself. "I'd been out with Reed Crandall, a gentleman of my acquaintance. He let me off and I went inside. There was no one out front, which I thought was odd since Mother or Father were always on hand when I wasn't. Then I looked behind the counter and saw her—"

Fargo stayed silent when she choked off. This was painful enough for her without him making it worse by pushing her.

"Blood was everywhere. My mother had been stabbed ten times, the doctor later informed me," Lorraine resumed. "I ran down the hall and found one of the boarders, his throat slit. Inside the next room was another." She closed her eyes. "Upstairs I found Father. He'd been cut the worst, but he was alive and trying to crawl downstairs to Mother."

"He told you who did it," Fargo said when she took a breath.

"Yes. A boarder who came in while I was gone. He gave his name as Skye Fargo."

This was the crucial moment, and Fargo was so intent on hearing her answer that he didn't notice when her eyes darted past him. "What did he look like?"

"Father said he was a tall man with dark eyes and scruffy clothes, and he hadn't shaved in a while."

"That's all?" Fargo asked, disappointed. The description fit half the men on the frontier and would be of no help at all in finding the guilty party.

"Just one more thing," Lorraine said. "The man smelled."

"Smelled?"

"Like he hadn't had a bath his entire life. Those were Father's exact words."

56

"It can't be," Fargo said, seeing in his mind's eye the mocking face of Wes Tucker and hearing again the man's demented cackle. Tucker hadn't been hungover when he claimed to be Skye Fargo. The man had been telling the truth all along, and Fargo had let the wily polecat slip right out from under his fingers. He had an urge to run to the Ovaro and go try to find Tucker's trail, which was a lost cause since Tucker would be long gone. As it was, the newcomer who suddenly spoke put an end to the urge anyway.

"What can't be, mister?"

The elated grin on Lorraine Knobel's face told Fargo he was in real trouble. He twisted and saw Sheriff Neal Barton holding a pistol on him.

"I hope you don't mind, ma'am," Barton said to her. "I've had a hunch about this hombre ever since I saw him in town. I watched him go in your place, and when I stopped by later you said he hadn't taken a room. So I figured he might show his face again, and he has." The sheriff was a wiry man who favored a handlebar mustache. His Colt was ivory-handled; his boots had been polished until they shone.

"But how did you know he'd turn up here?" Lorraine inquired.

"I didn't," Barton answered. "You were the honey that would draw the fly, so I was shadowing you."

Lorraine moved to the left. "I don't understand. Are you saying that you knew he would look me up? Why? Who is he?"

Sheriff Barton moved toward her. "Don't you remember the description Mitchem gave me? Big fella, lots of muscles, wearing a beard. The kind that turns a woman's head. Wears a white hat and buckskins—"

The lawman got no further. Lorraine Knobel's face contorted with loathing and turned scarlet. Her mouth worked but she only sputtered. Then, screeching like a she-cat in heat, she launched herself at the man she believed murdered her parents.

Fargo saw it coming and tensed to meet her charge. She waded into him with her fists flailing, and when he blocked the blows, she changed tactics and tried clawing his eyes out. She would have succeeded, too, except for the gloves she

57

wore. He grabbed her wrists to keep her from hitting him, which served to enrage her more. Howling fiercely, she kicked and bit and jabbed with her elbows.

"Lorraine, stop it!" Sheriff Barton cried.

The daughter wasn't listening. Growing madder moment by moment, she went positively berserk, and Fargo was unable to hold her at bay. She cuffed his lip, his ear. She tried to bite his neck, scraping his skin when he shoved her aside in the nick of time. Her claws dug into his throat, prying deep, her weight tottering him backward.

The sheriff was becoming concerned, but not concerned enough to lower his Colt. "Damn it all, Lorraine!" he bellowed. "Quit that this instant! I'll run him in and you can cheer at his hanging, if you want. But this isn't the way to behave."

Lorraine thought otherwise, as she demonstrated by driving her knee at Fargo's groin. By sheer chance he shifted enough to cause her to miss, his thigh flaring with pain where the blow landed. She was a handful, yet the whole time he struggled, Fargo kept one eye on the sheriff. He saw Barton hesitate, then move to separate them. Spinning so his back was to the lawman, he seized the front of Lorraine's dress as a hand tapped him on the shoulder.

"That's enough, mister. Let go of her and I'll take it from here."

"Whatever you say," Fargo said, and whirled, flinging the woman into the sheriff.

Barton had no hope of avoiding her. Tangled together, they crashed down beside the headstone of her father. The lawman wound up on the bottom, his gun arm pinned. He heaved to throw Lorraine off, but she slipped onto his legs. Barton sat up, raising his pistol, then stopped moving upon finding his nose almost touching Fargo's Colt. "Damn!" he said.

Fargo took the sheriff's pistol and stepped back.

Lorraine was halfway to her feet, riveted in place in horror. "Oh, God! Now you'll kill us like you did my folks!"

"Calm down, lady," Fargo responded. "I'm not here to kill anyone. All I want to do is get at the truth. You said yourself that your father gave you a different description than the sheriff was given by Mitchem. Which one is the right one? Which man was more reliable?"

"Before you answer," Sheriff Barton interjected, "there's something you should know, Lorraine. Mitchem was found dead in an alley last night, stabbed to death."

The woman's legs gave way and she sat back against the headstone. "It was you, wasn't it?" she accused Skye. "You came back to kill him because you knew he could identify you, and you want to kill me because you know I won't rest until you're swinging from a gallows for your heinous crime!"

"You have it all wrong," Fargo said.

"Prove it!" Lorraine said. "Give Neal back his gun and let us get up and leave and I'll believe you."

Fargo shook his head. "I can't do that."

"Figured as much," Lorraine spat.

Sheriff Barton displayed a more sensible attitude. "What *do* you plan to do with us, Fargo? If you're innocent like you claim, you aren't going to kill us."

"First I want some answers," Fargo said. "How soon after the killings did Mitchem come forward?"

"The next day, as I recollect," Barton said. "I was all set to issue circulars based on the suspect Lorraine's father described when Mitchem waltzed into my office and told me he'd just heard the news and wanted me to know that he knew you and had seen you the night before, right there at his table."

"And you believed him?"

"To be honest, I didn't know what to believe. Vince Mitchem was a shady character. He'd strayed into town about six months ago and stayed on as a faro dealer. I never much liked the man, but so long as he kept his nose clean in my county and wasn't wanted anywhere, I didn't care about his past." Barton paused. "I suspected there was more to his coming forward than he let on, but I had no idea what it might be."

Fargo squatted so that anyone passing on the road wouldn't notice him holding a gun on the local law. His next question went to Lorraine. "Was Mitchem close friends with your family?"

"Be serious. We didn't associate with such riffraff."

Nodding, Fargo shifted to the sheriff again. "Why didn't you issue a wanted poster?"

"I didn't know which description was the right one. Tom Knobel was more trustworthy, but he was weak from loss of blood and half out of his head when Lorraine found him. And Mitchem was so damned insistent he knew you. So to be on the safe side, I just wired to all the towns within fifty miles, asking them to be on the lookout for anyone calling himself Skye Fargo."

"That about answers everything," Fargo said, standing. He stepped a few paces toward the trees and stopped to wedge the sheriff's pistol under his belt. "I'll be taking this with me so you don't get any ideas. Wait ten minutes and you'll find it in that stand."

Lorraine rose to her knees. "Are you letting us live?"

"Be serious," Fargo mimicked her, then faced Barton one last time. "What can you tell me about the Jefferses?"

"Frank and Bob? What the hell do those two assassins have to do with anything?"

"Maybe nothing. Maybe everything."

Barton scratched his chin. "Well, I know as much as anyone else, I reckon. They've killed more people than all the badmen in Texas put together. Men, women, kids—it doesn't make a lick of difference to them."

"Do they always ride alone?"

"So far as I know."

"Where were they raised?"

"You mean the town they hail from?"

"That's exactly what I mean."

"Sawtooth. Every lawman knows that."

A few more pieces of the puzzle fell into place. "I'm sorry for the inconvenience," Fargo said, backing off. "Sheriff, I'd be grateful if you'd spread the word I'm not the man you want. Tom Knobel was right. You should be looking for a smelly son of a bitch who goes by the name of Wes Tucker—when he's not using my name."

"Now hold on," Barton said. "You shouldn't go after him by yourself. That's a job for the law. Turn yourself in and I promise you'll be treated decently until I sort things out."

"Nothing doing," Fargo said. The mere notion of being cooped up in a jail for days or weeks was enough to give him the jitters. "The next time you see me I'll have Wes Tucker along, and you can sort it out then."

"You're making a mistake."

"I've made them before." Fargo doffed his hat to Lorraine and half turned. "Be seeing you."

"Wait!" she called out, rising. "I'm going along."

Both Fargo and the sheriff responded at the same time: "Like hell you are!"

"Like hell I'm not!" Lorraine stated. "It was my parents who were murdered. I have more right than anyone to help bring in the man who did it."

Barton snorted. "You're being ridiculous, girl. Tracking mankillers is no business for a woman. And even if it were, how do you know you can trust this man? He seems honest enough, but looks can be deceiving."

"I'll take my chances." Lorraine walked toward Skye. "You're taking me with you whether you want to or not, mister, so you might as well get used to the idea."

"Go home," Fargo advised, and went to leave a second time. To his surprise, Lorraine ran over to him and grabbed his arm.

"Listen to me, please!"

"There is nothing you can say that will make me change my mind," Fargo said, while prying her fingers loose. "Do as the sheriff wants. He'll escort you to town."

"You can't do this to me!" Lorraine said shrilly. "If it were your parents, no one could stop you from going. If I were a man, you'd probably take me. But just because I'm a woman, you won't even hear of it." She snatched his sleeve. "You're not being fair."

Lorraine elevated her hands to the heavens in an impotent tantrum. "Help me!" she wailed.

Fargo rolled his eyes and walked on, covering five more yards before she tried again by shouting his name.

"I'm warning you! If you don't permit me to come, my blood will be on your conscience!"

"Don't listen to her!" Sheriff Barton said.

"I mean it," Lorraine shrieked as Skye ignored her and continued walking. "I'll outfit a packhorse and go after this Wes Tucker by myself. Don't think I won't! From one end of Texas to the other! And sooner or later he'll hear about me and decide to pay me a visit. What happens then, Mr. Fargo, will be on your head and yours alone, because you weren't man enough to lend me a hand when I needed it."

Stopping, Fargo glanced at the lawman. "Would she?"

"She would," Barton replied. "I've known this woman since she was knee-high to a pony, and she's always been headstrong. Wouldn't go off to school in the East like her folks wanted. Wouldn't marry the man they wanted her to marry. She's as independent as they come."

"You're crazy, lady," Fargo told her bluntly. "Wes Tucker, or whoever he is, will kill you in a minute if he thinks you're a threat to him."

Lorraine Knobel threw back her shoulders and grinned smugly. "Not if you're there to protect me, he won't."

"For all you know, I could be in cahoots with him."

"I trust my intuition, and my intuition tells me you're not the scum I thought you were. So what do you say? Will you take me along? I promise to keep out of your way and not interfere. And I'll cook for you on the trail."

Under ordinary circumstances Fargo would not think twice about her proposal. But he saw the look of anxiety the sheriff wore and the blazing determination in her eyes and knew beyond a shadow of a doubt she would do as she claimed. She was either too naive to truly realize the danger she would be in, or she simply didn't care. It was bad enough her independent streak would put her at odds with a slimy snake like Wes Tucker. Throw the two Jeffers brothers into the mix and she was just plain asking to be planted in the plot next to her parents.

With a female's awareness of such things, Lorraine seemed to sense he was weakening. "I won't slow you down, if that's what you're thinking. Ask Neal. I can ride as well as any man, and I'm a fair shot with a rifle."

Barton nodded once, then frowned, upset he had automatically confirmed her statement. "All that may be true," he said, "but you're biting off more than you can chew, Lorraine, if you go." He appealed to Fargo. "Damn it, mister. Tell her. You have the look of a man who has been up and down the river more than a few times. Convince her to stay put in King-fish where she belongs."

"That's right," Lorraine said angrily. "Put the female in her place. Shoo her back into the kitchen where she belongs. Never mind the justice of it all. Never mind that her mother and father are lying six feet under us and the man who did it is as free as can be." She moved toward Skye, her expression pleading more eloquently than her words. "Please!"

A tiny voice deep within Skye Fargo was hollering at him, telling him that he knew better, that he'd be better off taking a flying leap off a cliff than agreeing to such a harebrained idea, yet when he replied, his own voice said, "All right, lady. You can ride along."

6

"Did you see the look on poor Neal's face when I took his horse?" Lorraine Knobel asked with a laugh. "I thought for a minute there he was going to throw his hat on the ground and stomp on it."

"So you've said. Three times," Fargo responded. They had gone less than ten miles from the cemetery, and already he regretted his decision to bring her along. The wash had long been left behind. They were in heavy-brush country east of Kingfish, a maze of thorny vegetation bordering the verdant prairie. He'd chosen the route because the ground was so hard they would leave few prints and the thorns would slow down pursuers. It also slowed them down, since he had to pick a path carefully in order to spare their mounts the ordeal of being cut unmercifully.

"I'm sorry," Lorraine said. "I am rambling, aren't I? But then, I've never done anything like this before. To me it's a great adventure."

"To me it's a matter of life or death," Fargo said, glancing around. She rode well for someone dressed in her Sunday best, the handbag she carried slung over he left elbow, the hem of her dress up around her knees, revealing a pair of legs any man would drool over. The flush of excitement in her cheeks added to her beauty. Fargo shook his head and faced ahead. He had enough problems without that.

The brush became thicker and higher, the thorns bigger and more numerous. Fargo went around a bend and reined up sharply to keep from colliding with a solid wall of wicked spikes. "Back up," he said to forewarn Lorraine. "We can't go this way."

"Have you ever been through here before?" she asked as she expertly guided the bay backwards to a wide spot where she could turn.

"Not this exact area, no."

"I've heard stories of men who lost their way and were never able to locate the trail out again. Is that true?"

"Tall tales, nothing more. The kind men like to tell around campfires late at night."

"Good. Because I'll be honest. I'm a little worried about going this way."

So was Fargo, but he wasn't about to let on. The thorn barrier formed a labyrinth few men tried to penetrate. There was no water, scant forage. Anyone who didn't find his way out within three days seldom saw the outside world again, since that was how long most could go with no food without weakening and succumbing to exhaustion. Only complete jackasses, or those on the dodge, braved the thornbush country.

There was another danger, a worse threat than the thorns, as Fargo was reminded on seeing a fresh set of hoof tracks, deep prints that crossed the path they were taking at a junction with another.

"There's someone else in here!" Lorraine said.

"No."

"But those tracks—!"

"Were made by a longhorn," Fargo said. "A bull, from the size of them. He went by within the past hour."

"Longhorns can be quite temperamental, can't they?"

"That's one way of putting it."

Later more tracks appeared, all different sizes, cows and calves, Fargo judged. The bull had a harem and would be prone to attack anything it regarded as a menace to their safety. In short, anything that moved. He loosened the Sharps in the saddle scabbard and rode with one hand perched on his Colt, always alert for vague shadows where none should be. At times he could see over the top of the brush barrier. At other times it was too high, even when he stood in the stirrups.

By the middle of the afternoon Fargo was hot, sweaty, and thirsty. He removed his bandanna to mop his face. As he doffed his hat to wipe the brim, he heard his companion give a school-girl squeal.

"Oh! Isn't he adorable?"

Gazing in the same direction she was, Fargo spied the head of a longhorn calf in a gap to their right. It watched them with interest, then did the last thing Fargo wanted it to do: The calf trotted toward them, tail swishing in friendly greeting. "Ride," Fargo said, taking off at a trot.

"Whatever for?" Lorraine objected, but she did as instructed, her dress flying higher up her legs, exposing thighs the color and texture of smooth cream.

Fargo was vexed to hear the calf bawl and see it hurry after them. He went around a bend, slowing so Lorraine could catch up. She did, but by outdistancing the calf she caused the animal to bawl louder, which resulted in an answering bellow from the depths of the thorns. Fargo shooed Lorraine past him as a crashing racket broke out and a large animal smashed through the brush toward them.

In moments the calf's mother burst into the clear to their rear. Head tossing from side to side, she discovered them and gave chase. While not nearly as huge as the bulls, longhorn cows were formidable in their own right, with long, sharp horns and hundreds of pounds of sinew packed onto their motherly frames. This one snorted and kicked up her heels, preparing to charge.

Fargo had his hand on the Sharps when deliverance came from an unlikely source. Around the bend came the calf, and on beholding its mother it uttered a louder bawl than before. The cow stopped on a hair, spun, and hastened to her offspring, giving Fargo and Lorraine time to make their escape. They rode for half a mile before Fargo felt safe enough to stop.

"My goodness!" Lorraine said. "What happens if we bump into a whole herd of those critters?"

"Someone will come on our bones in a few years," Fargo said, tying his bandanna back on.

"How soon until we're out on the plain again?"

"Soon, I hope," Fargo said. Then he did something he rarely did. Giving the Ovaro a firm pat on the crest of its neck, he slipped his boots from the stirrups and raised both legs while slowly pushing on the saddle horn. The Ovaro shifted its front legs to accommodate the shift in his weight. Once he had his knees resting on top of the saddle, he held his arms out from his sides and rose to his full height. There had to be a healthy rapport between a man and his horse before a rider dared try such a stunt, as only the most dependable of mounts would tolerate the pressure on their spine. The stallion stood meekly, unbothered.

Fargo could now see for hundreds of yards in all directions. To the north and south were endless expanses of brush and thorns. To the west, perhaps a quarter of a mile away, lay the prairie. He smiled and said, "We're home free." But he had spoken too soon. For as he bent to straddle the saddle, to the east the vegetation crackled and snapped as an enormous dark shape plowed through it with an ease born of years of experience and a hide as tough as nails.

"A bull has caught our scent," Fargo divulged as he dropped on the saddle. He inserted his boots in the stirrups and leaned over to give the bay a smack. "Head west as best you can."

Lorraine tried, the constant twists and turns slowing her down, her arm raised to ward off branches that might tear her face or eyes. She paid no mind when a limb caught in her swirling dress and ripped the lower third.

Fargo pulled the Sharps on the fly, then inserted a cartridge. The Colt was useless. It would no more stop a bull than would a slingshot. And he had to make the first shot count, because rarely did a man have the luxury of a second. Longhorns and grizzlies were a lot alike in that they both were harder to kill than any other animal in the entire country.

Whether Fargo and Lorraine lived or not depended on whether they reached the plain ahead of the longhorn. It might not pursue them into the open, since wild bulls seldom leave the security of their thornbrush domain, where they are able to roam unseen, protected from men and beasts alike.

To Fargo it was obvious they weren't going to make it. Lorraine had yet to come on a path leading out, and the bull was closing rapidly. He could see the dark outline of its massive form as the vegetation splintered under its mashing hooves. When Lorraine came to a fork and bore left, Fargo elected to go due north, slowing as he turned and twisting to shout, "This way! Pick me, you bastard! Me!"

The longhorn slowed, its great head with the enormous six-foot spread of horns swiveling from side to side as it made up its mind which one of them it would chase.

Fargo decided the matter by shouting again, the noise drawing the furious bull on. Now Fargo had to ride in earnest, pushing the Ovaro to its limits, heedless of the thorns slashing at his flesh. Behind them the bull at last exploded onto the trail, snorting mightily, covering the ground with incredible speed for a creature so immense. Full-grown longhorn males sometimes weigh upwards of one thousand pounds, with a belligerent temperament that matches their size, and this one was typical.

Fargo galloped around another bend. The bull, though, took a shorter route, smashing straight through the brush, narrowing the distance between them by half.

The faithful Ovaro realized the danger and fairly flew along the winding pathway. Fargo always kept one eye on the longhorn, his thumb on the hammer of the Sharps. So it happened that he was a fraction of a second late in realizing the stallion had taken another bend and blundered into a dead end. The Ovaro dug in its hooves, sliding to within a hand's width of the thornbrush. Glancing back, Fargo saw the bull's bulk fill the opening. It was only fifteen yards away. Stopping, the monster bellowed, pawed the ground, then shook its head in mindless ferocity, its nostrils flaring as it puffed and fumed.

Fargo wheeled the Ovaro, but only partway. He angled the pinto so that it was broadside to the longhorn and slowly raised the Sharps to take precise aim. He hoped the bull would stand there a few more seconds, but he had no sooner touched the stock to his shoulder when the longhorn bawled a challenge and launched itself forward with the quickness of a feral cat.

A lesser rider would have lost his life then and there. Fargo still held the reins, dangling loosely in his right hand, but he made no attempt to tighten his grip and use them. Rather, he relied on his legs alone, on the pressure of his knees and a deft jab of his heels, to galvanize the stallion into action.

The Ovaro seemed to sense what was expected of it. As the longhorn bore down, the pinto stood as if smitten with fear. Then, at the very second it appeared the bull would bowl the Ovaro over, Fargo poked his spurs into the stallion and it leaped clear as spryly as a jackrabbit.

The longhorn whipped its horns, trying to gut the pinto, but merely succeeded in creasing the saddle. Fargo felt the tip of one horn brush his pant leg as the bull thundered past. He raced for the gap and the longhorn, unable to stop, barreled into the brush.

Fargo galloped around the bend, his last sight of the bull its hind end receding northward. He fully expected the brute to whirl and come after him. Leveling the Sharps, he waited for the longhorn to reappear. Given they were as unpredictable as rabid wolves, he didn't know which direction it would come from.

About ten feet back, the wall of vegetation on the right side suddenly buckled and out rushed the longhorn. Fargo managed to take a bead on its head, but as he went to squeeze the trigger, the Ovaro negotiated another turn. He tried holding the rifle steady but it was impossible. When the bull reappeared he had to compensate, swinging the barrel a few inches to the left. Once more, just as he was set to fire, another turn spoiled his aim.

And so it went for the next minute and a half. Fargo let the Ovaro run as it wanted. He had no idea where he was in relation to anything else, let alone the prairie, when to his heartfelt gratitude the pinto shot along a straight stretch and out onto open grassland. Fargo lowered the Sharps and brought the Ovaro to a gallop, confident he could now outdistance the bull.

The gigantic longhorn was descended from persistent stock. It pursued Fargo for over sixty feet before it drew up short, as if surprised to find itself on the prairie. Looking around, the bull snorted, pawed the earth once, then turned and trotted back into the depths of its prickly dominion.

Skye Fargo drew rein so the Ovaro could catch its breath. He eased the hammer down and replaced the rifle. Dismounting, he examined the pinto from ears to hooves, finding plenty of shallow cuts and nicks but no severe wounds. A bellow from the thornbrush made him suspect the longhorn had changed its mind and he swung up again. The monster never showed.

Nor did Lorraine Knobel. Fargo scoured the prairie bordering the brush and saw a single antelope to the southwest. It was the only living thing. He figured that he hadn't gone more than half a mile after they separated, so she should be somewhere close by. Puzzled, he clucked the pinto into a canter.

It soon became apparent Lorraine had disappeared. Fargo worried she might have gone back into the brush after him and tried telling himself no one would be that dumb. He came to where he believed she had left the thornbrush, and sure enough, the tracks of her bay were clear as day. The prints led westward. Fargo trailed them a few dozen yards to the lip of an old buffalo wallow rimmed by prairie-dog holes. Lying below were Lorraine Knobel and the bay, Lorraine with blood seeping from a nasty gash on her forehead.

Jumping down, Fargo scrambled over the side of the bowl and knelt at her side. The bay kicked weakly, lying in a spreading crimson puddle. Its right foreleg was broken, literally shattered in two spots, jagged points of bone jutting from the skin.

Lorraine groaned as Fargo examined her wound. Her eyelids fluttered, then snapped wide open and she gazed up at him in confusion. "Who—?"

"Skye Fargo," he reminded her. "We're on our way to find the man who killed your parents. Your horse stepped in a hole and threw you." He brushed bits of grass from her cheek. "You were lucky there was a wallow handy to land in."

"Now I remember!" Lorraine said painfully. She rose on an elbow and saw her mount. "Oh, dear! Look at all that blood! Will Neal's horse live?"

Fargo frowned and shook his head.

"He'll never forgive me. He loved that bay."

"Let's worry about you," Fargo said, to take her mind off the animal. "How do you feel?"

"Never better," Lorraine said, smiling. To prove her point, she tried to stand, but only rose as high as her knees before she whined in torment and pitched forward. She would have fallen on her face had Fargo not been ready to catch her. Nestling her head in his lap, he patiently waited for her to revive.

"I want the truth this time. How do you feel?"

"Poorly. As if my brain had been stomped to mush by a

stampede. There's a ringing in my ears and I have a hard time thinking."

"Damn. You might have a concussion."

"Meaning you're going to take me back to Kingfish?" Lorraine asked plaintively. "I won't go, I tell you! I'll resist every step of the way. You promised I could ride with you, and I'm taking you at your word!"

"Simmer down," Fargo said. "All it means is that we have to hide out for a few days, until you're fit to travel." Bending, he slid one arm across her back and the other around her hips. She tensed, blushing despite her condition, and pushed on his chest.

"What are you doing? How dare you put your hands on me without my permission."

"You're in no shape to walk," Fargo noted gruffly, lifting her with ease. Choosing a point where the side of the wallow had collapsed, he walked out and around to the Ovaro. "Rest a moment," he advised, setting her down gently. Lorraine regarded him quizzically, even though the reason he had to return to the wallow was self-evident. He didn't explain. She would know soon enough.

The next task wasn't one Fargo relished. Killing a fine horse never was. He made short work of the deed, then collected the lawman's rifle and a box of ammunition from the saddlebags. The saddlebags themselves, the saddle, and the bedroll had to be left behind, so he cached them under a pile of dry grass. The first town he hit, he would wire Sheriff Barton.

Lorraine studied his face as he approached. "You don't seem to have enjoyed that," she said, sounding surprised.

"Who the hell would?"

Fargo stuffed the extra ammo into his own saddlebags, then tied the Henry behind the cantle on his saddle. Stooping, he scooped her up before she could object and swung her onto the Ovaro. She swayed and clutched at the apple to stay on. Fargo put his hands on her left hip to hold her in place while he stepped into the stirrups and settled down behind her. "Comfortable?"

"No. I'm rubbing against the saddle horn. And our bodies are touching. It's unseemly. We should be farther apart."

"Unless you can figure a way to ride on the head and for me

to sit on the tail, this will have to do." Fargo skirted the wallow, heading out across the plain. He had gone barely ten feet when she let out a screech.

"Wait! My handbag!"

"What about it?"

"I must have dropped it when I took my spill. Please, let's go back. I can't get by without it."

"Buy yourself another after this is over."

"No. I implore you!" Lorraine looked back at him, entreaty in her eyes. "It has things I can't do without. My money, for one—unless you plan for me to rely on your hospitality for the duration of our journey."

Certain she would complain for the rest of the day if he failed to comply, Fargo circled to the wallow, searched the ground from horseback, and on locating the handbag, leaned way down to grasp the strap.

Lorraine gave him a look of heartfelt joy and tucked the purse to her bosom, as if welcoming a long-lost boon companion. "Thank you, Mr. Fargo. You have no idea how important this is to me."

"Can we go now, or did you lose your bloomers, too?"

"Has anyone ever told you that you can be downright crotchety at times?"

"Not in the last ten minutes." Fargo scanned the prairie. The nearest trees were miles away and would take the better part of the afternoon to reach.

"I didn't count on this when I asked to come," Lorraine groused as they resumed their quest.

"Were you expecting a picnic?" Fargo responded. "We're after a man who butchers people for the sheer hell of it, and we'll be going through territory no one except badmen and Indians call home. This is nothing compared to what will happen later on." Fargo looped his left arm about her slender waist to keep her from falling.

"If you're trying to scare me off so I'll beg to be taken to Kingfish, it won't work," Lorraine said. "I'm a lot tougher than you or anyone else thinks. So don't worry, mister. I'll hold out for as long as it—"

Her words dwindled to silence and she suddenly slumped to

the right, unconscious, her head resting on her chest. Fargo tightened his hold and chuckled. "No doubt about it. She's as tough as oatmeal."

Hawks and sparrows and buffalo were all that shared the plain with Fargo over the next few hours. The first stand of trees lacked a spring, so he went on to the next, and the next. The sun had changed from yellow to blazing red and crowned the western horizon when he entered an isolated tract of mesquite and discovered a small pool. A narrow shelf of bare earth flanked it.

Fargo had a campsite. He spread out his blankets and made Lorraine as comfortable as he could, his saddle her pillow. She stirred when moved but did not awaken, which he read as a bad sign. Covering her to her chin, he went off and presently shot a rabbit. He hoped the aroma of roasting meat and boiling coffee would bring Lorraine around, but she was as motionless as a log, as pale as paper. After filling his belly, he felt her brow and cursed under his breath.

Lorraine Knobel was in grave condition. She had a high fever and was caked with perspiration. Fargo took a spare bandanna, dipped it in the spring, and applied the folded compress to her forehead. He filled his tin cup, pried her rosy lips apart, and allowed water to trickle into her mouth. She moved her tongue but did not show any other signs of life.

That night Fargo slept little. He was up every hour or two to check on her, to change the compress and give her more water. She had changed from hot to cold—so cold that by the middle of the night her teeth chattered, even though he had a small fire crackling warmly at her side.

Morning brought the fever back. Fargo tended her, then stretched to relieve cramps in his legs. He strolled through the mesquite to clear his head, spooking a doe. At the edge of the mesquite he conducted a sweep of the prairie, paying particular attention to their back trail. He did not really expect to see anyone, since he was sure he had shaken off any pursuers in the thornbrush, so he was doubly surprised on spotting a half-dozen men jogging in tireless single file toward him.

Hunkering down, Fargo tried to identify them, but they were too far off. As the sun climbed and more sunlight bathed the plain, he distinguished rifles and bandoliers. He also saw bows and quivers and headbands. It was an Indian war party.

7

Skye Fargo automatically drew his Colt and slid back into the mesquite, where he could observe the warriors unseen. He eliminated Comanches as a possibility, since Comanches never went anywhere afoot. They were so fond of their warhorses they often kept the animals in their lodges at night. The band might be Apaches, he reasoned, although they seldom ranged so far east of their haunts in the Chiricahua and Dragoon Mountains. That left the Navajos—although the same argument applied to them.

Whoever they were, they were right on the Ovaro's trail. Fargo had to discourage them from getting any closer. He sprinted to the spring, grabbed the Sharps, and made it back to the boundary of the mesquite when the six warriors were within three hundred yards. The warrior in the lead was stooped over reading the sign.

Fargo worked the trigger guard, which levered outward, lowering the breechblock. He slid a cartridge into the chamber and pulled the trigger guard closed. Placing one knee flat, he propped his left elbow on the knee to steady the Sharps. Since his sights were set for one hundred yards, he had to adjust them for the extra distance.

The warriors were two hundred and fifty yards out when Fargo aimed with calm deliberation. He would give them one chance and one chance only to go earn coup elsewhere. The second Indian carried a shiny new rifle held in the crook of an arm. Fargo sighted on that rifle, lightly pulled the front trigger of the Sharps to set the rear trigger, and, after holding his breath and his arm rock-steady, he fired.

The second Indian jerked and staggered, his new rifle flying

74

from his fingers. All six men immediately went to ground, hiding themselves in the high grass.

Fargo inserted a new cartridge, then changed position, going five yards to the right in case the muzzle flash and gunsmoke had given him away. His display of marksmanship should convince the Indians to leave well enough alone, but there was no telling how they might react. He concentrated on the top of the grass, looking for stems moving against the breeze or jiggling back and forth.

Indians were masters at being stealthy. So Fargo was not the least bit surprised to finally see a cluster of grass shake less than fifty yards out. Upset they had not taken the hint, he aimed low, near the bottom of the cluster, and stroked the trigger.

At the booming retort, an Indian leaped erect, hand pressed to his chest, and took several faltering strides. He collapsed, arms outflung, and cried out.

Fargo reloaded, then changed position once more. The prairie remained undisturbed for the next half an hour. He stayed put another thirty minutes to play it safe. Hurrying to the stream, he found no change in Lorraine's condition. He did not like to leave her alone and unprotected, but he had to verify the war party was gone.

Vaulting bareback onto the stallion, Fargo took a roundabout route to the end of the mesquite. Once there, he bent low and rode in a wide loop, hunting for the Indians. No shots rang out, no war whoops sounded. At the cluster of grass a smear of blood marked where the warrior had fallen. From the manner in which the surrounding grasses were bent, Fargo determined that two others had crawled to the wounded man and dragged him off.

Drops of blood brought Fargo to where the Indians had first gone to ground. A piece of broken stock testified to his accuracy. The busted rifle was gone, as were the warriors.

Fargo surveyed the grassland and saw no evidence of them. Satisfied they had given up, he returned to the mesquite, to the spring, and knelt next to Lorraine. Her fever held steady and she breathed heavily. He made broth from leftover rabbit, then carefully force-fed her.

For the rest of the day Fargo hovered over the helpless woman, always there when she tossed and turned, always ready with a moistened bandanna to soothe her hot skin. That evening he shot an antelope at four hundred yards.

Another night of ministering to Lorraine left Fargo exhausted by morning. He rekindled the fire, made a circuit of the mesquite to insure no more unwanted visitors were in the vicinity, and sat beside her so he would be right there if she needed him. Toward the middle of the morning he could no longer hold his eyes open. He dozed.

A sound brought Fargo out of a sound sleep and he sat bolt upright, his right hand diving for the Colt. The fire had dwindled to embers. Close by the Ovaro grazed, unconcerned. He blinked, rubbed his eyes, and felt a cool hand touch his wrist.

"How long have I been out?" Lorraine Knobel asked. Her eyes were clear, her features restored to their usual healthy glow. She pulled the top of the blanket down and rubbed her throat, then stared at the sweat on her fingers as if it were a fungus, frowning in feminine disgust.

Fargo smiled. "Seems like forever."

"Feels like it, too," Lorraine said. She ran a hand through her tangled mat of hair and commented, "I must look a sight. And I sorely need a bath."

"You need food more than anything else," Fargo amended. He quickly prepared a haunch of antelope, skewering it on a makeshift spit over the fire. He also made a fresh batch of coffee. While the meat cooked, he cleaned the bandanna for the umpteenth time and brought it back to her. "This will have to do until you can take a dip in the spring."

Lorraine wiped her neck and face, her eyes never leaving him. "Have you been watching over me the whole time?"

"You make it sound like years. It was only two days."

"Two days!" Lorraine sputtered, forgetting herself and trying to sit up. She was not quite strong enough and sank back with a gasp. "I thought I was out a few hours, at the most." Again her eyes darted to his face, questioning, wondering. Her right arm disappeared under the blankets and roved down her body.

Fargo did not know whether to be amused or insulted. He

acted as if he hadn't noticed and turned the spit. "I figure you'll need another day to rest up. Then we'll head for Sawtooth."

"Why there?"

"The man who impersonated me at your boardinghouse was headed there, the last I knew."

"Isn't that where Sheriff Barton said the Jefferses are from?"

"He did."

"What's the connection?"

"I won't know that until we get there." Fargo tested the coffee by touching the pot. "Another few minutes yet." He saw her hand emerge. She shook her head in baffled disbelief, then folded both hands on her chest and was deep in thought. "I would have taken off all your clothes and washed you," he baited her, "but I didn't want you trying to blow my brains out when you woke up."

For some reason, Lorraine glanced at her handbag, which Fargo had put near her head. "You've been a perfect gentleman," she said, her tone implying she had anticipated the opposite. "If you were the man who murdered my folks, you would have finished me off while I was defenseless."

"Or at the very least," Fargo smirked, "I would have taken advantage of you."

Lorraine blushed guiltily. "All right. I'm convinced. You're not the one. But why did that gambler claim you were?"

"He was paid two hundred dollars by the man we're after, Wes Tucker, to make sure the blame was pinned on me. Tucker didn't count on your father living long enough to give a description of him."

"Why is this Tucker out to get you?"

"I wish I knew."

Soon the coffee was ready and Fargo offered her his cup, filled to the brim. When the antelope meat was well-done, he stuck a large chunk on the end of a stick and gave it to her. "Take small bites," he said. "Don't wolf it, no matter how hungry you are, or you'll get sick."

"Yes, sir," Lorraine said, and laughed—the first time she

had done so since they met—a full, lusty laugh that relaxed the lines of tension in her lovely face.

Fargo munched on some meat, debating whether to propose an idea that had cropped up when she first mentioned coming with him. She became aware of his scrutiny.

"Why are you looking at me like that? Is something the matter?"

"You should be married."

Freezing in the act of taking a bite, Lorraine flinched as if someone had jabbed her, then said, "Just when I was starting to think you weren't the ruffian you appear to be! You have your gall. My personal life is none of your business." She wagged the stick at him. "And for your information, I've had more than my share of proposals. I just haven't met the man of my dreams yet."

"Can't find one rich enough?"

"How dare you!" Lorraine shook the stick at him, nearly losing her meat when it started to slide off. She angrily crammed the chunk back on and gouged her palm on the tip, which served to make her madder. "Money isn't important at all! I'm looking for a man with certain qualities. He has to be a man of culture, well-mannered, sensitive to my needs, and with a sweet disposition."

"Sensitive? Sweet?" Fargo repeated, and chuckled. "Oh. I see. What you're really saying is that you want someone who will worship the ground you walk on. You want a man who is housebroken."

"I said no such thing!" Lorraine huffed. "Oh, you can be so infuriating!"

Fargo winked and said, "Has anyone ever told you how pretty you are when you're mad as hell?"

Speechless with indignation, Lorraine shifted, turning so she would not have to look at him. "You are an insult to your gender, Mr. Fargo. And exactly the sort of man I wouldn't marry in a million years."

"Too bad. And here I was thinking of asking you to be my wife." Fargo took a big bite and chewed lustily, acting as if he didn't see the amazed expression she bestowed on him.

"You must be insane!"

"I've been called worse," Fargo grinned. "I just thought it might be fun to be mister and missus for a few days."

"A few days?" Lorraine exclaimed.

"Maybe a week at the most."

"I would sooner mate with a lizard! There isn't any reason on heaven or earth why I would consent to such a ridiculous proposal!"

"Not even if it helps us catch the man who killed your parents?" Fargo responded, and went on while he had her undivided attention. "The man we're after is canny. If he gets one whiff that someone is hunting him, he'll dig a hole so deep we won't ever find him. Especially if word gets around that someone answering my description is asking a lot of questions about him." He held up a hand when she went to interrupt. "But Tucker won't be as suspicious of a husband and wife doing the same. He'll be more curious than anything, and might give himself away."

"Oh. You want us to pose as a married couple in order to catch this man." Lorraine pondered the suggestion. "It might work, but just how far are you willing to carry this marriage business?"

"We'd have to act the part or we won't fool anyone," Fargo said while eating. "We'd walk around on the streets making a display of ourselves, holding hands, that kind of thing. And we would need to share the same room."

"Now hold on—"

"Just for appearances' sake," Fargo emphasized. "You could take the bed and I'd sleep on the floor. And we would put up a curtain so you would have your privacy."

"I don't know," Lorraine hedged. "How do I know I can trust you to behave yourself?"

"You were lying there for two days and I didn't do anything," Fargo reminded her. Unable to resist having some fun at her expense, he added, "Besides, you have no cause to worry. You're not the type of woman I'd be interested in."

"Why not? What's wrong with me?"

"Nothing," Fargo said, drawing the Arkansas toothpick so he could slice another succulent piece of meat from the haunch. He made himself a mental bet that she wouldn't be able to let the matter drop, and won.

"Can't you be more specific? Most men find me quite attractive. I'm surprised you don't."

Fargo bit off a juicy tidbit and smacked his lips, enjoying himself. "I suppose I'm more partial to blondes. And I like women with a little more flesh on their frames. You're so skinny around the waist, I could fit my hands around you."

Lorraine puffed up her cheeks like a chipmunk about to go on the warpath. "Most men would find that a flattering trait. As for blondes, everyone knows they have nothing between the ears." She gave her tangled black tresses a pat. "I guess I shouldn't be surprised that someone like you prefers dumb women."

"And clean," Fargo said. "Don't forget, I like my women clean."

Predictably, Lorraine gazed at the spring. She finished her meal in silence and by then had enough strength to sit up. "I'd like to wash up now, if you don't mind."

"Go right ahead." Fargo gestured at the water. "Don't let me stop you."

"A gentleman would leave until I was finished."

"I could just turn my back," Fargo said, and had to fight hard to keep from cackling when her jaw muscles twitched a few times.

"A gentleman would respect a lady's privacy," Lorraine stressed.

Sighing loudly for her benefit, Fargo rose, taking the Sharps. "If I see one, I'll let him know." He hiked to the plain and idled away the time plucking grass while watching a small herd of buffalo.

Lorraine was tidying the blankets when Fargo returned. She had done wonders with her appearance. Her hair was combed and shiny, her dress as neat as if she had laundered it. She looked at him defiantly, challenging him to criticize her appearance, but he was too wise to take the bait.

For the rest of the day they made small talk, mostly about Lorraine's childhood. She had been an only child, the pride and joy of her parents. Never once did she directly refer to them. The conversation danced around their murders, and Fargo did not upset her by bringing up the deaths.

Supper consisted of more antelope. Fargo ate a light meal and made a final check of their retreat before turning in.

Lorraine was combing her hair again. "I'll be ready to ride out in the morning, if you want."

"So soon?"

"Trust me. I don't need another day. And the sooner we reach civilization, the sooner I can soak in a nice, hot tub and have my hair done properly."

"I wouldn't call Sawtooth civilized."

"Why not?"

"You'll see."

The town was as remote a settlement as any in Texas. Established by outcasts and misfits who were unwelcome everywhere else, Sawtooth had grown over the years to boast a population of four hundred. Saloons lined every street—so many that a newspaperman once claimed Sawtooth had more dens of iniquity than any town of similar size anywhere in the country. The stage now came twice a week, its sole connecting link to the outside world.

Reaching Sawtooth on horseback was a chore in itself. The country was dry, springs few and far between. The road was no more than a rutted dirt track winding among mesquite and boulders.

Fargo rode with care, leaving the road whenever riders approached. He explained to Lorraine that it would be best if no one saw them until he had a chance to buy a change of clothes. In town his buckskins would stand out like the proverbial sore thumb, and Tucker would have no trouble spotting him. He needed new duds to play the part of a married man.

Fargo had another reason for them to pretend they were husband and wife. If, as he believed, Frank and Bob Jeffers were somehow involved, he had to allay the suspicions of the two killers and their many friends and relatives. Sawtooth crawled with partisans of the Jefferses who would lose no time in relaying the news of a lone stranger asking about them. As a married man just passing through town, he could show mild curiosity without alarming anyone.

Lorraine grew subdued the closer they came to their destination. She wouldn't talk for hours at a time. Seated behind him now, she kept one hand on his shoulder and the other on her large handbag. "What do you do for a living?" she unexpectedly asked as they passed a crudely painted sign informing them the town was two miles further.

"Scout for wagon trains, break trails for herds, track when the need arises, go on a manhunt now and then," Fargo said. "Whatever suits me at the time."

"You're your own man, in other words?"

"I like to think I am."

"There have been no women in your life?"

Fargo grinned and skirted a hole in their path. "Never said that," he answered. "Fact is, no one could ever accuse me of being a monk."

"No permanent woman, I meant."

"I'm not in the market for one," Fargo said. "I doubt marriage is in the cards for me. The kind of life I live, I'll probably die young, but with a big smile."

"Thinking of all those blondes, eh?"

"I was joking you," Fargo said. "Blondes, brunettes, redheads—they're all the same to me." He paused, wishing he could see her face when he went on, "Since I'm being so honest today, I should let you know that you're one of the most beautiful women I've ever come across, and I've come across a lot."

"You're just saying that," Lorraine said.

"Meant every word."

By the time they came to another sign announcing they were only a mile from their destination, Lorraine had her arm loosely clasped around Fargo's waist and her cheek resting on his back.

Eventually Sawtooth came into view. Fargo left the road, riding around a boulder the size of a stagecoach. He reined up in its shadow and helped Lorraine climb down.

"Why are we stopping here?"

"We'll go in shortly before sunset when fewer people will be out and about." Fargo swung off and faced her. "And I'd like to take a look in that purse of yours first."

At the mention of the handbag, Lorraine placed it over her stomach and covered it with her hands. "Whatever for?" she asked innocently. "There's nothing in here that would interest you."

"Let me be the judge." Fargo held out his right hand. "Fork it over."

"I will not," Lorraine objected. "These are my personal effects. You have no right rummaging through them."

"There is only one thing I want," Fargo said. She took a step backwards and he lunged, grabbing the dangling strap. Lorraine twisted, then yanked to try and tear it loose. Fargo got both hands on the strap, and when that proved to be of no help, he gripped her wrist and pried her arm from the bag.

"Don't!" Lorraine said, struggling. "Why do you think I came all this way? I need it!"

"Sure you do." Fargo backed her into the boulder. She went to skip aside but he was faster, pressing his body against hers, pinning her in place. A flush that had nothing to do with their wrestling match crept up her face. He held her in place with his shoulder and slowly unwound her fingers from the bag.

"You can't!" Lorraine said, pleading.

Fargo flipped the leather flap up and without ceremony dumped the contents. Amid the shower of womanly paraphernalia was a glittering derringer, a Remington sporting ivory grips. She made a stab for it but he beat her again and held the parlor gun under her nose. "Do all respectable young Texas women go around packing hardware?"

"I carry it for protection," Lorraine explained lamely.

"And for shooting Wes Tucker dead the moment you see him." Fargo slid the Remington into a pocket. "I can't allow that, not until I learn why he wanted the murders blamed on me. There has to be someone else involved, someone who put him up to it. Once I've learned who it is, you can turn Tucker into a sieve for all I care."

Lorraine stared at the bulge in his pants. "You really mean that? I thought you needed him to testify."

"Your testimony will be enough," Fargo said. "Which is why I can't let anything happen to you." He was going to elaborate on his notions involving Tucker when the Ovaro pricked its ears. He put a hand on the pinto's muzzle, keeping it quiet as riders passed by on the road. Warily, he stepped to where he could see them, a trio of hardcases in grubby clothes.

"I wouldn't care to be alone with those three," Lorraine whispered in his ear.

Fargo turned, and for a few seconds they were nose to nose, mouth to mouth, her warm breath caressing his lips. She looked into his eyes, then gave a toss of her head and retreated a pace, seemingly frightened.

The moment of closeness had set Fargo's blood to racing. He walked to the Ovaro to check the cinch, and to calm himself. There was a time and a place for everything, he reflected, and this sure as hell wasn't it. He had to be at his best when they entered Sawtooth and had to stay alert the whole time they were there, or neither of them would ever leave.

To the west, the sun steadily sank lower.

8

"I think you look downright handsome," Lorraine Knobel said seriously. "If I was interested in you, I'd be flattered to have you at my elbow. Not that I am. Interested, I mean."

Skye Fargo stared at his reflection in the store mirror and squirmed uncomfortably. He had worn buckskins for so long that the sight of himself in store-bought clothes made him think he was looking at someone else. The stiff collar on his black shirt and the tight-fitting jeans reminded him otherwise. "If you say so," he muttered, gazing longingly at his folded buckskins on the bed.

"This was your idea, as I recall," Lorraine said. She chortled at his expense.

"Let's make the rounds," Fargo proposed, taking her elbow. He guided her to the door, locking it behind them. "Do you have the story straight?"

"We're on our way to San Antonio," Lorraine recited. "We stopped over to search for my brother. The last our family heard from him, about five months ago, he was living here."

"And don't forget your brother's good friend, Wes Tucker," Fargo said. She offered her arm, so he took it as they walked down the stairs to the lobby of the Lone Star Hotel, the only lodging quarters in Sawtooth. The clerk, a rodent of a man who wore spectacles, lit up like a candle, his beady eyes feasting on Lorraine's ample cleavage.

"Good evening, Mr. and Mrs. Lewis. Taking some evening air, are you?"

"Why, yes, Mr. Bristol," Lorraine responded. "Should anyone come by about my brother, please take a message."

"I certainly will," Bristol promised, adjusting his red tie.

"And if there is anything else I can do for you, anything at all, you have but to say the word."

"My, aren't you charming!" Lorraine shook Fargo's arm. "Isn't he charming, dear?"

"Don't overdo it," Fargo growled under his breath. He pulled her away from the clerk, who all but blew her a kiss, and walked out onto the boardwalk. Darkness claimed the town, broken by the golden glow of windows and a few flickering lanterns outside the busier establishments. Strolling to the right, Fargo nearly collided with a man coming from the other direction. He opened his mouth to snap a warning for the fellow to watch where he was going, when to his surprise the stranger smiled ever so sweetly and tipped his hat to Lorraine.

"My, my. Aren't the folks here friendly?" she said.

The man went on around, almost tripping over a chair because he couldn't tear his eyes off her.

"And you claimed this would be a dangerous place for me," Lorraine teased.

"Keep it up and it will be," Fargo blustered.

The nightlife of Sawtooth was coming alive. Saloons lured in customers with the merry laughter of fallen doves and the lively melody of music. Eateries had signs out front advertising their specials of the day. Most of the town's inhabitants were single men, but there were a few married men as well, and Fargo saw several of them doing exactly as he was doing, sharing a walk with their wives. He imagined himself taking the same stroll, night after night after night, and shivered.

"What's the matter?" Lorraine asked.

"It'll be a cold day in hell before I tie the knot."

"What's gotten into you? All because a woman flirts a little?"

"Never mind."

It was safe to say that every male they passed turned to ogle Lorraine. Fargo had to put on a show and act as if he never noticed, when deep down he had half a mind to pistol-whip the bunch of them. He would never have thought it possible, but he found himself in sympathy with married men who resented having their wives treated like so much prime beef on the hoof.

At last the ordeal was over. They had made their circuit and were in front of their hotel once more. Fargo slid his arm from hers and said, "In you go, dear. And don't wait up."

"Where the dickens are you off to?"

"To make my rounds of the saloons. By now half the town must have heard about us, so I can mingle freely."

"And what am I supposed to do while you're off having fun? Sit in our room and twiddle my thumbs?"

"Twiddle whatever you like," Fargo said, grabbing her shoulders and turning her toward the entrance. "Just don't set foot out of our room. And keep the door locked at all times." He gave her a swat on the fanny and she spun, streaking her hand aloft to slap him. "Remember," he said quickly, waving a finger under her nose, "we're man and wife now. It wouldn't do for you to slap your husband in public."

Lorraine mumbled a few choice words, shot lightning bolts from her eyes, and stormed inside. The desk clerk sang out to her and was given the same treatment. Her dress crackling like her temper, she bustled up the steps.

Fargo glanced at the startled clerk. "Women!" he said, and laughed. Hitching at his gun belt, he walked to the nearest saloon. A cloud of cigarette and cigar smoke hung thick below the rafters. At the bar stood a dozen drinkers; at tables men played poker and other games. No one seemed unduly interested in Fargo as he bellied up to the bar and ordered a whiskey.

The bartender, a barrel-chested man with more hair than a bear, brought over a stained glass and a half-full bottle. "New in town?" he asked casually.

Fargo gave the story he had concocted about seeking Lorraine's brother. "Art Daniels is his name," he finished. "The name ring a bell?"

"Can't say as it does, and sooner or later I get to know most of those who live hereabouts."

"Maybe you know a friend of his, then. Someone named Wes Tucker?"

"Never heard of him, either."

And so it went. Over the next several hours Fargo visited every watering hole and whiskey mill he could. Everyone he talked to told him the same thing. None gave him the impression they were lying, which forced him to conclude Tucker was an alias. His scheme was fast unraveling. He would have to cook up another way of tracking Tucker down.

The desk clerk was dozing in a rocker when Fargo reached the hotel. Climbing the stairs three at a stride, he rapped lightly on the door to the room, wondering if Lorraine would admit him or if she was so mad she would make his sleep in the lobby with the snoring clerk. The bolt rasped softly.

Lorraine was scooting into bed. She had tried to unlock the door and get under the covers before he came in, but was a tad too slow. She wore the skimpiest of lacy pajamas, which she must have bought earlier when she purchased a new dress.

Fargo caught a glimpse of jiggling breasts and of the dark triangle of hair at the junction of her thighs. She ducked under the covers, raising them to her chin, and stared at him as if he were there to molest her.

"Your blankets are all laid out."

The chill in her tone left no doubt as to whether she had forgiven him. Fargo discovered she not only had spread his bedroll, but also had strung a blanket next to the bed as a partition. He removed his boots and gun belt, and sat.

"Did you learn anything?" Lorraine asked hopefully.

"Not a damn thing."

"What do we do next?"

"Your guess is as good as mine." Fargo peeled off his new shirt and hat and lay back, a hand propped under his head. He stared at the ceiling, pondering their next move, and noticed a cobweb in one corner. A fly had blundered into it some time ago. Now it struggled weakly, while nearby sat a big brown spider, watching and waiting.

Fargo reflected that if not for a whim of fate, he would have met the same end the insect would face shortly. He had almost been snared in someone else's web of lies, almost lost his life to the guns of the trigger-happy citizens of Ripclaw. But unlike the fly, he had escaped—temporarily, at least. And unlike the fly, he had no idea who was behind the effort to see him dead. "Who is the spider?" he mused aloud, as was his habit on the trail when he had no one else to talk to except the Ovaro.

"What?" Lorraine Knobel piped up.

"Nothing," Fargo said. "Just thinking."

"Any ideas?"

Fargo had no chance to answer. Heavy footsteps sounded outside, and their door shook to the hammering of a fist. In a twinkling Fargo was on his feet, the cocked Colt in his right hand. He padded to the right of the door. "Who is it?"

There was no answer.

"Who the hell is there?" Fargo demanded.

"Be careful," Lorraine said.

Nodding, Fargo quietly worked the bolt, then yanked the door wide open as he crouched with the Colt extended. An empty corridor mocked him—empty, that is, save for a folded sheet of paper lying close to the door. He warily looked both ways, insuring it wasn't a trick.

"Who is out there?" Lorraine wanted to know.

Fargo picked up the paper, locked the door, and stepped to the edge of the bed. He unfolded the sheet. The message was short and to the point: *Stop asking so many questions. Leave town on the stage tomorrow or you will be leaving in a pine box. A friend.*

"We don't have any friends here, do we?" Lorraine asked over his shoulder. She had slid forward to see the note for herself.

Fargo glanced around. The blanket had slipped partially off, revealing most of her enticing right breast. He could just make out the rim of her nipple, and the sight set his loins to twitching. Oddly, she seemed not to be aware of the effect she was having. "None that I know of," he said.

"What will they do when we don't leave as they want?"

"Maybe you should," Fargo commented.

"I beg your pardon?"

"Maybe it was a mistake for me to bring you along," Fargo said. "The men we're up against play for keeps. They had this warning delivered because they don't think we're much of a threat, yet. Just too nosey for our own good. But if they figure out who I am, or what we're up to, they won't hesitate to kill us."

"I knew the risks when I asked to come."

"So did I when I agreed. Knowing them and facing them are two different things, though. Maybe you should head out on the afternoon stage. I'll deal with this alone from here on out."

"Nothing doing," Lorraine said harshly. "I won't rest until the bastard who butchered my parents is right where he belongs. You try going it alone and I'll hang around to spite you. I mean it," she vowed somberly.

"I don't want your death on my conscience."

Lorraine blinked, and apparently by accident the blanket dipped even lower, fully exposing both breasts. "Why, Skye Fargo, I didn't think you cared," she said, grinning.

Fargo let the paper fall. He twisted, placed his right hand on one gorgeous tit, and gently squeezed. She sucked in a breath and stiffened but made no attempt to push his hand away.

"What do you think you're doing?"

"Exactly what you want me to do," Fargo said, putting his other hand on her other breast. She squirmed, licked her lips, and placed her slender palms on his broad shoulders.

"What if I asked you to stop right this second?"

"I'd stop. But you don't want me to."

Lorraine cocked an eyebrow. "You think you know women, don't you?" She paused, her eyelids fluttering when he squeezed both breasts hard. "You're always so damn sure of yourself. What if I told you I don't want to make love to you?"

"You'd be lying." Fargo squeezed again, and suddenly she moaned and swooped her moist mouth to his. Her tongue darted between his parted teeth, entwined with his tongue in a silken coil. He took her nipples in the tips of his fingers and mildly tweaked them, eliciting a hungry growl deep in her throat. The blanket slipped all the way off as she locked her fingers in his hair.

Fargo knelt in front of her so they were chest to chest. The lacy garment fell at her knees, revealing her womanly charms in all their glory. With her chest rising and falling, her breasts firm and hard, and her mouth open in wanton anticipation, she was stunning beyond words. He kissed her again, feeling her nipples mash his chest. His right hand stroked her glossy thighs, working inward inch by gradual inch. Her stomach quivered with rising intensity as her nails raked his shoulders and arms.

Fargo eased her backward onto the bed. She was supple, soft, smooth—her ardor matching his own. To his delight, she slid a hand to his groin and lightly rubbed his manhood through his pants. He reciprocated by sliding several fingers between her legs, to her moist crack. Lorraine groaned, her pelvis pumping at the slightest touch. When he found the tiny knob at the core of her being, she cried out, softly, and opened her legs wider.

With his finger and his thumb, Fargo drove her to the heights of ecstasy. He knew just where to rub, knew just how to move to incite her lust. Soon she gushed, shaking like a leaf while tossing her head from side to side. He inserted another finger, which made her pant huskily.

Her kisses were like the sweetest of nectars, her scent intoxicating like liquor. Fargo lathered her breasts, her throat. He nibbled a path from her cleavage to her navel and from there to the border of her black thatch. She rolled her eyes, pumping against him in a harbinger of things to come.

Fargo's pole was rigid with desire, straining against his trousers. He quickly removed the rest of his clothes, then lay flush on top of Lorraine with the tip of his member brushing her womanhood. She wriggled her bottom, trying to ease his pole inside of her, but he held himself still to prolong the suspense.

"Please," Lorraine whispered. "Oh, please."

"All in good time."

Fargo sucked on an earlobe while rubbing her breasts. He ran a hand over her ribs to her hips, and from there to her inner thighs. She pulsed with passion, her legs rubbing him without letup. Fargo cupped her buttocks to hold her still, then with painstaking patience glided his throbbing organ into her wet sheath a fraction of an inch at a time.

"Yes! Yes!"

Balanced on his elbows and knees, Fargo commenced a rhythmic thrusting, slowly at first but with increasing urgency.

His mouth found hers and stayed there. Her legs went around his waist, her ankles locked behind his back. She acted desperate to attain the pinnacle and pumped with fervent abandon in an attempt to incite him to greater speed, but he was in no rush.

Fargo rose on his hands, using his arms as levers to gain more power for his strokes so he could penetrate her deeper. She looped her wrists behind his neck, her head slack as she wheezed and cooed, lost in the delirium of total passion. Fargo pecked her cheeks, her brows. Her mouth opened and her tongue protruded. He sucked it into his mouth, thrusting harder still.

They reached the summit simultaneously. Fargo was driving into her like a piston, his arms and legs corded masses of muscle, when a tingling at the base of his spine forewarned him of the inevitable. He went faster and faster, matching his thrusts to the beating of his heart. The eruption sent a shiver of pure pleasure through him. Lorraine bucked and heaved, groaning loud enough to wake the clerk in the lobby. She held on tight, her own eruption coming moments later. To keep from shrieking, she bit his shoulder, her teeth gouging deep enough to draw blood.

Together they coasted to a stop. Fargo slumped on top of Lorraine, her heaving breasts cushioning him. She grinned and lazily twirled his hair with a finger.

"And to think I didn't let you do this sooner!"

"It doesn't change a thing," Fargo said, easing to her side. "If you're smart, you'll leave tomorrow like they want."

"Never. You might as well get used to the notion of having me around for the duration."

"That's what I was afraid you'd say," Fargo grumbled, nuzzling her neck. She responded with a kiss and cuddled against him. Fargo tried to stay awake to debate the point, but lassitude gripped him and he drifted into dreamland with his arm draped over her.

The next thing Fargo knew, sunlight warmed his eyes. He awoke to find dawn an hour gone and Lorraine already awake and staring at him with the same questioning look she had given him once before. "Morning. How long have you been up?"

"Not long." She scooted off the bed and over to the closet. "Let me tidy up first. Then the wash basin is all yours." Smiling, she hurried off with a new dress over her arm.

Fargo spent the time mulling over how best to proceed, now that he'd run up against a dead end. Somehow he must learn Wes Tucker's real identity, which wouldn't be easy with the locals so tight-lipped. Sawtooth lacked a lawman; nor was there a great need for a newspaper when three fourths of the population couldn't read. Those avenues were denied him. And since the saloons had proven a waste of time, he had but one avenue left.

It was past eight when Fargo strapped on his gun belt and turned to Lorraine. "Ready for a late breakfast?"

"I thought you'd never ask. I'm famished."

The town could boast of seven eating establishments, in large part because the majority of single men would rather eat anyone else's cooking than their own. The nearest to the hotel was also the fanciest. A plump waitress in a neat pink uniform came to their table, pencil poised above her pad.

"What will it be, folks?"

Lorraine had been studying the menu. She went to order, but Fargo held up a hand, cutting her off. "Just coffee," he said.

"Coming right up."

As the waitress flounced off, Lorraine pushed Fargo's hand to the table and gave him a hard pinch. "Why did you tell her that when you know darn well I could eat a horse?"

"You'll get your chance. Don't worry."

"What are you up to now?" Lorraine asked.

"You'll see."

When the coffee came, Fargo turned on the charm, leaning toward the waitress and smiling. "I bet it must be hard being on your feet all day and having to deal with customers who couldn't make up their minds if their lives depended on it."

Surprised by his interest, the waitress nodded. "Mister, you don't know the half of it. I could tell you stories you wouldn't believe. This job can be a nightmare at times."

Fargo nodded in understanding and gave her hand a pat. She acted as if she had been touched by royalty. "You do get to meet a lot of people, though," he went on. "That must be nice."

"It can be," the waitress said, her tone suggesting a world of possibilities. She gave Lorraine a haughty look.

"Maybe you've met the man we're looking for," Fargo said, and gave a fake description of the fake Art Daniels.

"Can't say as I have."

"Then how about his friend?" Fargo pressed. "A tall man with brown eyes, who wears a shabby beard and favors dark clothes?"

"There must be dozens who answer to that description, honey."

"This one smells worse than most."

The waitress's smile died. So did her pleasant manner. "I've got work to do. Excuse me." She walked off, giving them both a glance that did not bode well.

Lorraine slid back her chair. "The hussy knows something, Skye. I say we question her. If she won't cooperate, I'll beat the truth out of her."

"Hold your horses, you bloodthirsty wench," Fargo grinned, trapping her arm under his. "Do that and word will spread fast. No one in town will give us the time of day."

"Then we're just wasting our time."

"Look," Fargo said, nodding at a table across the packed room.

The plump waitress was whispering to a slovenly fat man and casting repeated glances in their direction. In a short while the man nodded, then paid his bill and hurried out.

"Who is he? Where is he going?" Lorraine asked.

"We'll find out soon enough. When our coffee comes, drink a little and we'll leave."

"Leave? Where to?"

"The restaurant down the street."

At each and every eating place Fargo asked the same questions, but at none did he get the kind of reaction he had at the first. At the last one Lorraine was able to indulge her appetite. On their way to the hotel she patted her tummy and remarked,

94

"All this food and exercise has me in the mood again. What do you say?"

Fargo was bemused by the change in her. "What happened to the shy woman who wouldn't let me watch her bathe?" he asked.

"And I thought you knew everything!" Lorraine gave him a playful squeeze. "Once you make love to a woman, all her inhibitions are gone." To demonstrate, she kissed him full on the lips. "So what do you say?"

"Normally I'd say yes, but first we have to deal with the man who is shadowing us," Fargo said. She began to turn and he poked her gently with his elbow. "Don't look or he'll know that we know. Act as if you don't have a care in the world."

"How long has he been following us?"

"Since the third restaurant." Fargo had noticed a gunman wearing a red bandanna peeking in at them through the front window, and ever since the man had dogged their steps. His brainstorm had paid off. Now he wanted to handle the next step alone. Once at the hotel, he escorted Lorraine to their room, then said, prior to opening the door, "Stay here until I come back. Hopefully this won't take long." He shoved the door wide and motioned for her to enter, then stiffened on seeing the room already occupied by a quartet of gunmen who had their pistols out. One was the fat man from the first restaurant, who smiled broadly and beckoned.

"Come on in, Mr. Lewis. We need to have us a little talk."

9

Skye Fargo did not even try to go for his own gun. To do so would be certain suicide, and would result in Lorraine's death as well. He thought of shoving her, of urging her to make a run for it, but the gunman wearing the red bandanna suddenly appeared at the top of the stairs, hand on his six-shooter.

"I'm waiting, Mr. Lewis," the fat man goaded. "And I don't like to be kept waiting.

Lorraine surprised Fargo by boldly going in first and raking the gunmen with a stare of utter contempt. "What is the meaning of this outrage, sir?" she demanded. "Harm us and I'll see that every one of you answers to the law."

"Spare me your threats, ma'am," the leader said. "There ain't any law within fifty miles of here." He rose off the bed and nodded at the gunman with the red bandanna, who had followed Fargo inside. The door was promptly closed. "Now then, the way I hear it, you folks have been all over town asking about a gent with the handle of Wes Tucker. That so?"

Fargo stepped in front of Lorraine so if there was any gunplay she would be behind him and less likely to be hit in the cross fire. "You know it's true, mister," he answered. "Just as you must know we're trying to find my wife's brother."

"The name is Reece," the man said. "And yep, I've heard that story, too." Reece rubbed the stubble rimming his pudgy chin. "Funny thing is, no one I know of has ever heard of any Art Daniels. And some of us have real good memories."

"Are you calling us liars, Mr. Reece?" Lorraine snapped. "I'll have you know my brother sent letters home from here."

"You wouldn't happen to have one of these letters, would you?" Reece asked.

The man had them and Fargo knew it. But Lorraine never batted an eye. "Not with me, no," she said. "Our mother has them all. Art was always dear to her, and she couldn't bear to part with the only remembrance she has of him."

"How touching," Reece said. He moved in a small circle around them, studying Fargo, his stride showing he was remarkably light on his feet for someone so heavy. "I'll take your word for it, ma'am. Just as you have to take my word that your brother never lived here, not for one day he didn't. So it would be best for all concerned if you were to stop pestering folks and get on the afternoon stage south."

"I'm not leaving until I find my brother," Lorraine insisted.

"Your choice," Reece said, halting by the door. "Just you remember this." He spoke sharply, jabbing a thick thumb at them. "So far we have been right hospitable, and let you snoop as you liked. But the men who run Sawtooth figure you've looked all you need to. Keep on searching and they'll take it as an insult. Then anything could happen."

"I'd like to talk to these men," Lorraine said. "What are their names?"

Reece chuckled. "Quite a few people want to know who they are, but they like to keep their names secret." He gestured, and the gunmen began to back from the room. "If you don't want any harm to come to your pretty wife," Reece told Fargo, "you'd be wise to do as you're told. This is your last friendly warning, friend."

No sooner had the door closed than Fargo dashed to the closet and pulled out his buckskins. He ran to the window to swiftly change while watching the front of the hotel. Reece and company emerged, then turned right, disappearing up the street.

"What are you doing?" Lorraine inquired.

"The first thing they'll do is go see whoever sent them," Fargo said. "If they don't lose me, they'll lead me right to him."

"What if they spot you?"

"They'll be looking for someone wearing a black shirt and jeans," Fargo said.

"There are five of them and only one of you," Lorraine complained. "Take me with you. I can shoot."

"Nothing doing."

Lorraine tried another tack. "I don't like being left here all alone. Think of what might happen if they come back while you're gone, or if they kill you. I'd be at their mercy."

Fargo finished dressing and tossed his store-bought clothes onto the chair. He had been thinking along the same lines, which was why he extended his hand, offering her the derringer. "Keep this at your side at all times."

"You trust me enough to let me have it back?"

"Your life comes first," Fargo said frankly, making for the closet again. Retrieving the Sharps, he hastened to the door, stopping when she clutched his arm and gave him a warm kiss.

"Take care, handsome."

Instead of departing through the lobby, Fargo bounded down the back stairs. A narrow alley brought him to a side street, where he turned and hurried to the main street. The five gunmen were nowhere to be seen, and he thought he had lost them until he saw them ride from the livery. Instantly he bent, fiddling with his boot while they went by.

Sprinting to the stable, Fargo soon had the Ovaro saddled and was heading out of town at the opposite end. He swung in a wide curve, and once Sawtooth was out of sight he galloped to overtake the gunmen. They had taken the dusty ribbon of a road to the southwest. From a hill he observed them trotting in a knot, the fat man in the lead.

Since Fargo and Lorraine had used that very road on their way into town and not passed a single house or ranch, Fargo was intensely curious to learn Reece's destination. He was certain the gunmen would lead him straight to Wes Tucker, and by nightfall the mystery would be solved.

Only five miles outside of Sawtooth the gunmen bore to the right along a well-worn trail. It took them into hilly country, the hills arid and barren. Fargo was hard-pressed to keep them in sight without being seen, but he succeeded, and toward the middle of the afternoon he saw them climb a ridge and vanish beyond. He approached the ridge cautiously, the Sharps across his lap. The slope was littered with loose rock that might clatter and give him away, so he dismounted and climbed, leading the stallion by the reins, picking his way to the top.

Fargo crawled the final few yards. He figured he would see more dry country stretching to the horizon. Instead, a small verdant valley watered by a meandering creek unfolded before his wondering gaze. The gunmen were nearing a ranch house set amidst tall elms. Elsewhere were catclaw and a few junipers. Horses and a few head of cattle grazed in a fenced pasture. The scene was so tranquil Fargo wondered if the gunmen were simply stopping at a rancher's to water their mounts. Then he saw the bunkhouse in the shadows, saw several men emerge to greet the new arrivals with handshakes and claps on the back. The horses were stripped and set loose in the pasture. All the men except one went into the bunkhouse. Reece walked to the main house and was admitted.

Fargo had to go down there, but not while the sun was up. He moved along the ridge to a boulder-strewn slope and there sought shelter from the baking sun. The afternoon waned. As the shadows lengthened, Fargo mounted and rode northward, seeking an alternate way into the outlaws' lair. Evening descended, bringing with it a welcome cool breeze from the northwest.

A game trail pockmarked by deer and antelope tracks provided the means of reaching the valley floor. Fargo halted at a small pool the wild animals drank at so the Ovaro could slake its thirst. From there he worked his way along the creek, never once venturing into the open. He saw lights come on in both buildings and heard the clang of the supper triangle.

Fargo was within hailing distance when he drew rein and tied the pinto to a bush. Leaving the Sharps behind, he crept along the pasture fence until he could see the bunkhouse clearly. Inside, a long table ran the length of the room, and seated there, eating hungrily, were eight or nine men. He skirted to the left, going all the way around to the rear of the main house.

A small yard fronted the back door. Inside was a kitchen. Through the window Fargo could see Reece seated at a table near a stove, talking nonstop while stuffing food into his mouth. Curtains prevented Fargo from seeing the man Reece addressed. He shifted to another position but still could not see.

Presently Reece mopped his mouth with the end of the tablecloth, rose with hat in hand, and walked out. A shadow flitted across the curtains, providing no clue to the man's identity.

Fargo drew the Colt. In a crouch, he sped across the yard to the door, flattening next to it. He tried the latch, found the door locked. Stymied, he stalked along the wall to the corner, passing a closed window which was also locked. He spotted Reece lumbering toward the bunkhouse. Retracing his steps, he went past the back door to the other corner, waited a suitable spell, then moved toward the front.

Inside the house someone whistled. From under the sill of a window to a darkened room, Fargo glimpsed someone walking along a hall. He ducked low, and light spilled out over him as a lamp was lit within. He could hear footsteps approaching the window. He glanced up, suspecting he had been seen, but there was no outcry. All he saw was a long, vague shadow on the pane. Then the footsteps retreated and a door closed.

Fargo tried the window and this time he was in luck. It slid upward, creaking slightly—loud enough for him to pause and listen before hooking a leg over the sill and easing inside. There was a settee, several nice chairs, and a bench in a corner. The walls were paneled. And to Fargo's surprise, in another corner stood a bookcase. He hadn't pegged Wes Tucker as the bookworm type.

Stepping lightly toward the door, Fargo was as tense as a fox in a chicken coop. The threat of discovery hung heavy in the air. He set each foot down slowly, thankful the polished floorboards didn't creak. At the door he pressed an ear to the panel. The house seemed quiet.

Opening the door a crack, Fargo gazed down the corridor toward the kitchen. He saw no one. Encouraged, he turned to gaze in the other direction and suddenly found himself looking down the barrel of a cocked shotgun. That in itself was unnerving. But the luscious redhead holding the gun on him was enough to take his breath away.

"Howdy, good-looking," she said with a smirk. "I'd lose

that hardware if I were you, unless you can live a normal life without a head."

Fargo dropped the Colt. At that range, if he tried anything, anything at all, she would put a hole in him the size of a watermelon. Raising his arms, he stepped back. She pushed the door open with the shotgun and entered, a mischievous gleam in her blue eyes.

"I should shoot you on the spot, but it's so seldom I have visitors. My brothers just won't allow men around me. They claim I devour men like sweet candy." She laughed. "Are you sweet, big man?"

Fargo had no idea who she was. Her friendly attitude led him to believe he might be able to talk his way out of the fix he was in, so he smiled and said, "Sweet as sugar, ma'am. And confused, too. It seems like I made a mistake. If you'll be so kind as to hand over my pistol and let me leave, I'd be grateful."

The redhead tittered. "Would you, now?" She gestured at a chair. "Sit while I think it over."

Obeying, Fargo folded his hands. "I don't mean you any harm," he assured her. "I was looking for someone else."

"Someone I know?" she responded gaily. The shotgun abruptly steadied on his chest. "Who might you be, mister?"

Fargo did not want anyone to know the truth. Nor did he care to incriminate Lorraine by giving the name he used as her husband. So he made up a new one on the spot. "Lee Harkey," he said.

"And who are you looking for, Mr. Harkey?"

"A man who calls himself Wes Tucker."

"Do tell." The redhead stepped to the Colt, bent at the knees, and scooped up the pistol without ever taking the shotgun off him. She handled the six-shooter like an expert, twirling it and banging two shots into the floor before Fargo guessed her intent. She waited a few seconds, then banged off two more shots.

A veritable stampede of boots pounded outside. Someone thumped on the front door. There were so many men shouting at once, Fargo couldn't distinguish the words.

"Come in, you peckerwoods!" the redhead bawled. She sat in another chair, the shotgun across her legs.

Fargo glanced at the window, tempted to make a break for it despite the certain outcome. He knew what he could expect from the likes of Reece and the gunmen.

"I wouldn't if I were you, handsome." The woman made a clucking sound. "There isn't a man alive who can outrun buckshot."

The corridor echoed with the thud of running men. They filled the doorway, Reece foremost among them, each with a six-gun in hand, some with fresh food stains on their shirts and chins.

"Mr. Reece," the redhead said, "meet our guest, Lee Harkey."

"Harkey, hell!" the fat man barked. "This is the one I was telling you about, miss. This is the husband, Lewis. He must have trailed us all the way here from town."

"Interesting," the redhead said. She tossed the Colt at Reece, who nearly dropped his own trying to catch it. "So they didn't take the hint and leave on the stage like we wanted. Too bad." Her rosy lips pursed. "Or did she leave and he stayed on by himself? Send Red and two of the boys into Sawtooth to see if the wife is still at the hotel."

"And if she is? Do you want us to haul her back?"

"No. Just keep an eye on her for now. Have them report to me at least once a day."

"Yes, ma'am."

Standing, the redhead stepped to the bookcase. "As for our curious friend here, truss him up for me. And don't be gentle, boys. I hate uninvited company."

The men spilled through the doorway, shoving one another in their eagerness to get at Fargo. They poured past the woman. Fargo was out of the chair like a shot and racing for the window, knowing she couldn't fire now without hitting them. He gained the jamb and was sticking his right leg through when a half-dozen hands fell on him and he was yanked off his feet. Punches rained down like hail. Kicks slammed into his sides, his head.

Fargo fought as best he was able, landing blows to the right and the left. The only thing that saved him from being battered senseless in the first few seconds was that so many men were trying to get at him at once, they got in one another's way and couldn't swing effectively. He saw a kneecap and slammed a heel into it. Knuckles raked his face. Another fist plowed into the pit of his stomach. Bruised and bloody, Fargo shifted, caught someone in the ribs with a right cross.

"Pin him!" Reece roared above the bedlam. "Pin the bastard down!"

Iron fingers locked on Fargo's wrists, his legs. He tore his right arm loose and hit a gunman in the mouth. Resist as he might, it was a lost cause, and within moments they had him flat and helpless, his limbs spread-eagled. Reece reared above him and raised his Colt on high.

"No!" the woman bawled. "I told you I wanted him tied up, not beaten to death!"

Reluctantly Reece lowered the Colt. "You heard her!" he snarled. "Lester, fetch some rope. And be quick about it."

They did a thorough job, lashing Fargo's ankles together first, then his knees, then his wrists, finally adding loops of rope around his upper arms. Reece tied most of the knots himself, and he took sadistic delight in making them as tight as he could. Finally the heavy gunman rose, nodding.

"That'll hold him, miss. Want us to string him up upside down from that big tree out back? Or maybe tie him out where the sun will bake his brains tomorrow?"

"No, Reece. This will do." The woman let down the hammer on her shotgun and walked over. "Homer and the others will want to question him themselves, which means he has to be in good enough shape to answer. The boys and you can go on back to the bunkhouse."

"Want me to leave a couple of men to guard him?"

"That's not necessary."

"But, miss," Reece protested, "your brothers will skin me alive if anything happens to you. What if he breaks loose and does you harm?"

The redhead laughed merrily and prodded the rope binding Fargo's knees with the toe of her boot. "Breaks loose? Are you joshing me? You have this hombre trussed up so, he can hardly wriggle a finger. He'd have to be Samson himself to break free. Don't worry. I'll be fine."

"Please, ma'am—" Reece refused to be pacified, but she held a hand up, silencing him.

"Are you saying I can't handle myself?"

"No, ma'am. I'd never be fool enough to say something like that."

"Then quit badgering me and go, before I lose my temper," the woman said. She added, as an afterthought, "And let me know when you find it."

Reece looked blank. "Find what, ma'am?"

"His horse, stupid. Or do you think he flapped his arms and flew all the way here from town?"

Several of the men laughed. Reece turned beet-red and glared at them, and they immediately fell silent. "You heard the lady," he rasped. "We've got us a horse to find. So move it, you coyotes!"

Fargo watched the gunmen file from the room and was gratified to see some of them nursing bruises and limping. Presently he was alone with the woman, who leaned the shotgun against the wall and came to kneel beside him. Up close, he saw a wild gleam in her eyes he hadn't detected before, a gleam that suggested underneath the beautiful surface lurked a fiery demon. She touched a spot on his forehead, making him wince.

"Does that hurt, good-looking?" she asked, grinning. "You do have a nasty bruise there. But don't worry. This is nothing compared to what my brothers will do to you when they get back."

"Who are these brothers you keep talking about?"

The redhead scrutinized him closely. "You really don't know, do you? You must be a lot dumber than you look." She paused. "My brothers are Frank and Bob Jeffers. I'm Cassandra Jeffers, their little sister."

No one had ever mentioned the killers had living relatives, but Fargo wasn't surprised. Many wanted men belonged to outlaw families, entire clans that lived life on the wrong side of the law and had no compunctions about doing so. When such outlaws were on the dodge, their relatives provided places to hide and shielded them from capture. Now Fargo knew where the Jefferses hid out when they were on the run and why no lawman had been able to find their lair. He remembered a statement Reece had made in town, and asked, "Does your family run things in Sawtooth?"

Cassandra seemed unduly interested in his face. She didn't answer right away, but instead ran a fingernail along his chin. "More or less," she said absently. "There are a few others who have a lot of say, but mostly they listen to us." Her nail traced a line to the tip of his nose. "You really are one handsome devil, you know that?"

Fargo saw the beginnings of a familiar hunger in her gaze, and could do nothing except lie there as she pushed off his hat and ran a hand through his hair. Grasping at straws, he said, "A beautiful woman like you, I bet you get your share of compliments, too."

"Not as many as I'd like," Cassandra said wistfully. "My damn brothers hardly ever let me go into town."

Fargo understood now. She was restricted to the valley, penned up like a prized thoroughbred, denied companionship. In short, she was man-hungry. More than he knew, because she suddenly reached down and grabbed hold of his manhood.

"My, my," Cassandra said, licking her lips. "I've seen stallions with less than you." A lecherous grin spread over her face. "You give me the nastiest notions, big man."

"Untie my hands and I'll see what I can do about satisfying them," Fargo said, hoping against hope she would take the bait. He should have known better.

The distaff Jeffers laughed lustily. "You must take me for an idiot, Lewis! If I let you get away, my brothers will beat me black-and-blue. No, you'll stay hog-tied until they return. Sometime tomorrow, I do believe."

Fargo felt her hand move as she stroked him through his pants. He had no conscious desire to give her satisfaction, yet his pole swelled anyway. Bound as he was, he could do no more than lie there helpless as she rolled him onto his back and hitched at his belt.

"Don't look so pained," Cassandra taunted. "It's not like

I'm fixing to hurt you or anything." The buckle came unfastened. "You'll like it. Trust me."

"What if someone walks in on us?" Fargo asked.

"I'm the only one at home. Reece and the others wouldn't dare set foot in this house without my permission." Cassandra undid his pants and slowly peeled them downward. "Mercy me!" she giggled. "I'm having Christmas early this year."

Skye Fargo resigned himself to the inevitable. Resting his head on the floor, he thought of Lorraine and the danger she was in, and of the Ovaro, which would soon be found, and he chafed at being bound. Then Cassandra's hot lips descended and an electric pulse tore through him. He could no more deny her than he could stop breathing. She aroused him to a fever pitch, to the brink and beyond, and he forgot about Lorraine, forgot about the stallion, forgot about everything except the fire in his loins and the exquisite sensation of Cassandra's molten lips.

10

It was the middle of the night when Skye Fargo opened his eyes and groaned. Cassandra Jeffers had drained him dry, not once but twice, doing things to him that hadn't been done since the last time he'd visited a bawdy house in Kansas City, plus a few more tricks the fallen doves had yet to learn. Adding insult to injury, she had left his pants open, his manhood fully exposed, and walked off giggling to herself.

That had been hours ago. Now Fargo lifted his head and discovered the door closed, the lamp burning low. He bent at the waist, tucked his knees to his chest, then, grunting, bent his legs so he could slip his fingers inside the top of his right boot and grip the hilt of the Arkansas toothpick. He had to tug and jerk to free the blade. Once he did, he sliced at the rope around his ankles, the razor edge making short shrift of the strands.

The rope around his knees was easier to cut since it had loosened a little during Cassandra's playtime with him. At length he rose, kneeling, and reversed his grip on the toothpick to work on freeing his wrists. Since he couldn't apply as much pressure, he had to slice long and hard before the rope fell off. Finally he removed the loops around his shoulders and rose, shaking his arms and legs to restore his circulation.

Fargo went to the door and opened it. Cassandra had left lamps lit all over the house, so he need not worry about bumping something in the dark as he glided down the hall toward the front door. He passed another room and paused to glance inside. Sprawled out in a most unladylike fashion was the mistress of the house, snoring like a drunken trooper. He went on to a living room. A gun cabinet drew his interest. It was unlocked, and inside were several new rifles and various pistols. He shoved a Colt similar to his own under his belt.

The front door opened noiselessly. Fargo recalled hearing someone pound on it during his interlude with Cassandra to report the gunmen had found his mount. Cassandra had lifted her head long enough to tell them to tie the horse and get lost. Sure enough, the Ovaro stood next to the hitching post. His saddle, saddlebags, and Sharps were all in place.

Not so much as a whisper came from the bunkhouse. The lights were out, the gunmen fast asleep.

Fargo had a lot to do. He crept back into the room where they had bound him and selected several long pieces of rope. Tiptoeing into Cassandra's bedroom, he moved to the bed and bent over her ankles. She mumbled and smacked her lips as he carefully eased her legs together and lightly looped rope around her ankles.

A noise outdoors made Fargo look up, but it was only the distant wail of a lonesome coyote. He tightened the rope. As he made the first knot, she stirred. As he made the second, her eyes fluttered. And as he grabbed her wrists to bind them, Cassandra snapped awake and tried to sit up, blurting, "What in the hell!"

Fargo held onto her arms, his knee across her chest. "Don't make this any harder on yourself than it will be," he cautioned.

Cassandra Jeffers's inner demon took full control. The gleam of madness came into her blazing eyes. Screeching like a panther, she tried to knee him in the groin, while at the same time she attempted to claw his face.

Fargo had to shut her up before she woke up the men in the bunkhouse. He tried clamping a hand over her mouth, but she bit his fingers. Her screeching grew louder, her resistance more fierce. With a short, powerful jab, he slugged her on the jaw and she collapsed, groaning. He had to work swiftly. Fargo tied her wrists, then rummaged in a dresser drawer until he found a handkerchief, which made do as a gag. Leaning down, he slung her over his right shoulder and hastened to the front door.

The coyote howled again as Fargo carried Cassandra to the Ovaro. He untied the reins and led the pinto to the pasture fence, where he deposited his burden and took his lariat in hand. The gate rails slid off quietly. Entering the field, he adjusted the loop of his rope and walked toward a dozing chestnut. The horse offered no resistance as he roped and brought it out.

Cassandra was coming around. She growled like an animal as Fargo lifted her, then thrashed wildly when he draped her over the back of the chestnut.

"Keep this up and I'll hit you again," Fargo whispered in her ear. She calmed, but he had no delusions about her staying that way.

Fargo swiftly mounted the stallion and led the chestnut into deep shadow at the side of the house. Dismounting, he ran to the front door and down the length of the hall to the kitchen. A lit lamp sat on the table. He hefted it, then flung the lamp at the base of the curtains adorning the window. The glass shattered, spilling coal oil. Flames leaped from the floor to the curtains, which burned rapidly.

Turning, Fargo hastened to the next room, and the next. In each he upended lamps. From the living room he took two more, one in each hand, and raced to the bunkhouse. He stopped in front of an open window. Inside, someone was asking if anyone had heard a noise. Fargo chuckled as he flung the two lamps and saw fire spread instantly.

Curses broke out, mixed with the crash of furniture. Fargo sprinted to the house. He rounded the corner and was reaching for the saddle horn when he realized no one was on the chestnut. "Damn!" he fumed, scouring the ground. He saw no one, but he did hear a rosebush near the far corner rustle. Dashing over, he found the redhead furiously crawling away.

Fargo was none too gentle as he slung her over his shoulder a second time and carted her to the horse. He threw her on, then mounted the stallion and headed toward the east side of the pasture.

Confusion reigned at the bunkhouse. The outlaws had poured into the night, many with nothing on but their underwear and their boots. Some had thought to grab buckets from a shed and were frantically dipping them in a water trough and heaving the water onto the rapidly spreading flames. Then one of the men realized the main house was on fire and cried out. In a body the gunmen sped to the front door and barreled inside, yelling for Cassandra.

Meanwhile, Fargo reached the middle of the east fence. Horses were scattered throughout the pasture, either grazing or sleeping. He angled the Colt at the sky, then squeezed off three swift shots and yipped like a Comanche. The spooked horses broke into a run, making for their sole avenue of escape—the gate.

The gunmen became aware of this new problem too late. Five or six ran to head off the fleeing horses but were unable to stop the animals from galloping pell-mell into the night.

Fargo glanced back at the redhead, who had craned her neck to witness the proceedings. She was snorting angrily and kicking her legs in rage. "If you think this is something, lady, you just wait," he told her. "Your family's days of murdering people are about over."

Cassandra glared at him. Reflected light from the fire danced in her eyes like the flames of hell itself. Her expression said it all. Given the chance, she would kill him—and relish doing so.

Clucking the Ovaro eastward, Fargo headed for the ridge. He figured it would take Reece's cohorts until dawn to round up all the stock, giving him a three- or four-hour head start. Not much, but enough if nothing else went wrong.

Taking the winding trail at night was a hazardous proposition. The darkness hid abrupt curves, holes, and ruts. Fargo had to exercise extreme care. He often relied on the stallion's instincts to get them around obstacles without mishap.

The pink blush of impending dawn streaked the sky when Fargo reached the poor excuse for a road. He stopped long enough to untie Cassandra's legs and sit her upright, warning, "Try anything and you'll regret it." She couldn't answer, but her eyes crackled with hatred.

Fargo pushed the horses until Sawtooth appeared. Twice he had to leave the road and hide while early travelers went by. Half a mile from the outskirts of town he entered a gulch and went up it a hundred yards, past a bend. Here he swung down once more and lifted the redhead off the chestnut. "I'll be leaving you a spell," he said. "If a bear or a cougar comes along, just look at it the way you look at me and it'll run off with its tail tucked between its legs."

Cassandra tried to speak, her words muffled by the gag.

"I know I shouldn't," Fargo said sarcastically, pulling the handkerchief out, "but I've always had a soft spot for a pretty face. What do you want?"

"You're a dead man, Lewis!" Cassandra hissed. "My brothers will make wolf meat of you for this outrage! They'll find you, you know! No matter where you go, how far you run. And when Frank and Bob are done, there won't be enough of you left for your precious wife to cry over!"

Fargo took the outburst in stride, then added to her aggravation by smiling. "You've got a few things wrong, Miss Jeffers."

"Like what?"

"For one thing, I'm not married."

"But Reece said—"

"We both know Reece couldn't find his own backside with both hands if he didn't already know where it was." Fargo began coiling the loose end of the lariat he had looped around the chestnut's neck. "The woman I'm with is after your brothers for the murders of her parents."

For the first time uncertainty etched Cassandra's haughty features. "That doesn't make a difference. My brothers will find you and kill you just the same."

"I want them to find me," Fargo said.

"What?"

"Did you think I'd gone to all this trouble to bring you along for your charming company?" Fargo laughed, and could have sworn steam came out of her ears. "No, I'm using you as bait."

"You're loco."

"Am I? No one else has ever been able to get close to your brothers because Frank and Bob always stay one step ahead of any posse. This time I'm one step ahead of them. I've got someone they'll want back. And as you keep pointing out, they'll follow wherever I lead."

Cassandra was troubled and it showed, but she put on an arrogant front. "So what? They'll get you in the end, Lewis, no matter how clever you think you are."

"That's another thing. My name isn't Lewis."

"Then what the hell is it?"

"Skye Fargo."

Disbelief made her recoil a stride. "You can't be!" she declared. Suddenly she lashed out, kicking his leg, and whirled to flee.

Fargo winced as pain flared up his thigh, but he recovered immediately and caught her in three strides. Holding her by the shoulders, he pulled her toward a cleft in the side of the gully. She resisted with all her might, stopping only when he tripped her and shoved her to the ground.

"You bastard! We've heard about you! The wife of that couple down in Waco told some of her friends and they told a newspaperman. Homer was down in Waco, heard the story the first day it came out!"

"Who is Homer?"

A crafty look came over her face. "He's the real brains in our family. Frank and Bob make all the headlines because they're so well known. But Homer has killed twice as many folks, and not a living soul knows about it."

"Was it Homer's idea to have me framed for murder?" Fargo asked, and saw he would get nowhere. The question closed her mouth tight. She held her head as if defying him to pry the information out of her, but he didn't bother. He gripped her jaw, forcing her mouth wide, and crammed the gag in while avoiding her gnashing teeth. Cassandra then attempted to kick him again. He sidestepped her feet, and a minute later had her bound at the ankles. "No wonder you don't have many men callers," he remarked. "With a disposition like yours, a man would have to be part grizzly to hold his own."

Cassandra coiled her legs and brought both heels down in an effort to smash his toes. Fargo skipped backward, then seized her by the front of her dress and dragged her to the cleft. "Annoy the bugs a while," he said, pushing her in. He made her as comfortable as he could and stepped back.

The lariat she had made him drop when she kicked him took

but a few moments to coil. Fargo placed the rope under a heavy rock so the chestnut couldn't stray off, then swung onto the stallion. "I won't be long," he said.

The redhead sputtered, as if trying to spit at him.

Sighing, Fargo rode down the gully to the road and trotted toward town. The sun had about cleared the eastern horizon and already many residents were abroad, mostly men scurrying for breakfast.

Fargo went past the hotel rather than stopping, shifting in the saddle so anyone out front would not get a clear glimpse of his face. He spotted a man in a gray duster lounging in the mouth of the alley on the near side of the hotel, another man smoking a cigarette while leaning against the corner of the first building on the far side. Neither showed much interest in him, as the street was filled with other riders and several wagons.

A block past the hotel, Fargo hitched the pinto. He wanted to get Lorraine out with as little fuss as possible. With the front entrance covered, he decided to try the back way. Going down the side street, he was in the act of turning the corner when he spied a small man in a red bandanna standing across from the hotel. It was the one nicknamed Red. They had her boxed in.

Backpedaling, Fargo returned to the main street and mingled with those on the boardwalk. He soon spotted the second gunman, the one leaning against the corner of the hardware store. The man faced the hotel. Fargo debated whether to try and slip past without being seen, then decided on another course of action upon spying a stack of seed bags outside the store. Ducking inside, he walked up to a bespectacled clerk. "I'd like to use one of your seed bags for five minutes. How much?"

The man glanced up from making notations in an account book. "I'm sorry. I must not have heard correctly. Those bags are for sale, not for anyone to use as they see fit. Do you want to purchase seed?"

"I just need to borrow a full bag," Fargo reiterated. "What will it cost me?"

"Borrow a bag of seed?" The clerk laughed, thinking it was a fine joke. "I've never heard of anything so silly."

Fargo glowered, his hand dropping to the butt of his Colt. He had no time for such nonsense, not when the outlaw gang might arrive at any minute. "One last time," he said gruffly. "How much to carry a bag of seed from here to the hotel and back again?"

The clerk finally realized the request was in earnest. He glanced at the Colt, then through the window at the burlap bags. "I must say, this is most irregular. But if you promise to bring the seed back, I'll let you use one for, say, one dollar."

"Highway robbery," Fargo grumbled as he forked over the money. Everyone in the store had heard the exchange and watched him walk out and heft the top bag to his right shoulder. He took a few steps, and hesitated. The first gunman, the one on the other side of the hotel, was staring across the street at a pretty woman. The nearer gunman was in the act of lighting another cigarette.

Striding brashly forward, the large burlap bag hiding his head, Fargo walked right past the smoker and into the hotel. The desk clerk stared at him in mild curiosity, which changed to outright amazement when Fargo dumped the bag on the counter with a thud. "Watch this until I come down," he said.

"But—" the man sputtered.

"I won't be long," Fargo said. "I just have to collect my wife." Pivoting, he started toward the stairs.

"But that's just it, sir!" the clerk declared. "Mrs. Lewis isn't in her room."

Fargo was at the counter in a stride. "Where is she?" he demanded in a tone that caused the clerk to drop the pencil he held.

Frightened, the man spoke in a rush, "I don't know, sir. I saw her go out to supper yesterday evening, but I can't remember seeing her come back." Glancing anxiously at the entrance, he spoke in a whisper. "And when I opened the lobby this morning, three men were waiting. They wanted to know if she was in. I didn't know what to tell them."

"What did you?"

The clerk seemed to be trying to shrivel into his clothes. "I didn't think they would believe me if I told them she wasn't, and I didn't want them tearing up the hotel looking for her." He coughed. "So I informed them that she was in, but that I would have to check with her before I let them go up."

"And?" Fargo goaded when the man stopped.

"That was the odd part. They said there was no need to bother her, and let it go at that."

"You did the right thing," Fargo said, running off. "I'll be right back." He had the Colt out when he reached the landing. The door was unlocked, a definite bad sign. His back to the wall, Fargo pushed the door open—or tried to, because it hit something on the floor and stopped. He kicked, forcing the door wider, and the top of an overturned chair poked into view.

Crouching, Fargo dived through the gap. He came up with the Colt leveled, but there was no need for gunplay. The room was empty. Someone had reduced it to a shambles, knocking over everything, tearing the bed apart, ripping the sheet. His new shirts and pants were in tatters, as were all of Lorraine's clothes except those she must have had on at the time.

Puzzled, Fargo walked around the room seeking clues. It made no sense for anyone to have taken Lorraine. The only ones who would do it were the outlaws, and they were watching the hotel in the belief she was still inside.

A commotion drew Fargo to the window. He saw people hurrying to get indoors, riders trotting off in either direction. He looked both ways but saw no reason for the exodus.

Eager to go find Lorraine Knobel, Fargo hastened toward the corridor. He was almost past the door before he noticed the note tacked to the back of it. Tearing the paper off, he read. *Just got back in town and heard you were asking about me. Invited your woman for a little talk. If you want her, come find her. Wes Tucker.*

Fargo's stomach balled into a knot. Tucker, or whatever the hell the man's name happened to be, would take sadistic glee in tormenting Lorraine. For all Fargo knew, she was already dead, her body dumped somewhere for the coyotes to feast on. Even if she was alive, he had no idea where to begin searching—and no time, either, since Reece and the gunmen would be arriving shortly.

Crumpling the note, Fargo threw it down and hurried to the lobby. Three steps from the bottom he heard a loud groan. Halting, he inched to the corner for a look.

The desk clerk lay sprawled in front of the front desk, a smear of blood on the carpet by his head. His glasses had been crushed under a boot heel. The seed bag lay on top of him.

Fargo scanned the lobby but saw no one else. Through the front window he could see the main street, which now appeared completely deserted. He had an idea why, and the idea sent an icy chill through him. Bending low so as not to draw fire, he went to the desk clerk. The man would live, but he'd have a headache to beat all headaches.

Walking in a crouch to the big window, Fargo scoured the town for a sign of life. There was none. It was as if every last resident had been whisked off by marauding Indians. Only he knew better. Suspecting what lay in wait for him if he went out the front, he hurried to the back door and eased it open wide enough to see the spot where Red had stood just ten minutes ago. Red was gone. Nor was there anyone else anywhere around.

Fargo closed the door and leaned on the wall. Tucker or Reece or both had him boxed in, front and back. They had spread the word, told everyone in Sawtooth to keep indoors until the shooting stopped. There was no way out for him except through the gauntlet of their guns.

In a situation like this Fargo could use the Sharps. He was sorry he had left the Ovaro so far down the street. It would be a miracle if he got halfway down the block, let alone reached the stallion alive. He worked the bolt, locking the rear door so his enemies couldn't get at him from behind, then walked down the hall. Nothing had changed, other than that the desk clerk had moved slightly.

Fargo darted across the lobby to one side of the entrance. He checked the cylinder, verifying he had a cartridge in every chamber, then gave the cylinder a spin and cocked the hammer. He didn't relish having to go up against so many killers. Necessity had given him a proficiency few men possessed, and his skill had often come in handy on the trail, but he wasn't one of those who lived and died by the gun, who sold their deadly skills with six-shooters to the highest bidder. He was a plainsman, a tracker, a scout, not one of the new, reckless breed who considered themselves gunfighters.

Turning, Fargo gripped the back of a chair and lifted it. He slid closer to the front window, then paused on seeing a face pressed to a pane across the street—the face of a young boy looking out excitedly for the show to commence. The boy saw him and ducked back in alarm.

Fargo decided not to disappoint the waiting populace of Sawtooth. Shoulders rippling, he whipped his body around and heaved the chair. The glass shattered, spraying out onto the boardwalk and the street. As it did, during that instant when the attention of every last gunman would be riveted on the window, Skye Fargo bunched his legs and bolted out the door.

11

The distraction bought Fargo all of five seconds. He was almost to the corner by the hardware store when the gunman fond of cigarettes popped out of the alley and snapped off a rushed shot that thudded into a post behind him. Fargo responded in kind, his slug catching the man high on the forehead and flipping him backwards.

More guns opened up on the other side of the street as Fargo raced past the hardware store window. Lead punched hole after hole in the glass, creating a spiderweb of cracks. Then Fargo was past the window and ducking behind a barrel. A rifle boomed, and the plank at his feet erupted in a shower of splinters. He saw a man at an upstairs window taking aim. Snapping the Colt up, he fired once. The rifleman stiffened as if impaled, his rifle clattering from his fingers, and pitched from sight.

Fargo had to keep moving. Bullets were kicking up dirt in the street, punching into objects to the right and the left, and smacking into the wall to his rear. He broke from cover, weaving and dodging, never going straight for more than two or three steps at a time. In front of him another gunman appeared, the one called Red, at the selfsame moment that a revolver cracked to his rear. Fargo dipped to one knee, firing twice from the hip, dropping Red, then whirled and fired once more, striking the other gunman in the chest.

Flinging himself behind a water trough, Fargo had to shield his face with a forearm as bullets ripped into the trough from all directions, sending wood chips flying. Water spouted from a dozen holes, soaking his shoulder, his neck. He rolled to the left, heaved erect, and ran on.

A shrill voice rang out above the din of guns from a saloon across the way. "Stop him, you stupid sons of bitches! I'll have your hides if you don't!"

It was Wes Tucker. Fargo glanced at the Ovaro, still tied at the end of the block, then at the saloon, which was much nearer, and did the last thing the gunmen expected. He changed course. Angling toward the saloon's batwing doors, he snapped off his last shot at a man in a black hat who appeared on the roof with a Spencer in hand. The man toppled, screaming.

Gun barrels suddenly burst through a window to the left of the doors. Fargo hit the ground, bullets thudding within inches of his body. Hurtling to the right, he rolled and rolled until he was at the corner of the building. He darted around the corner and crouched, listening to the crack of revolvers and rifles, their number greatly reduced.

Fingers flying, Fargo reloaded the Colt. He would much rather have his own. The one he had was better than most, finely balanced, the trigger light to the touch. Shoving in the sixth cartridge, he slapped the hinge shut and risked a peek. The gunfire had stopped. There was movement in the saloon, the crash of furniture and the sound of a bottle breaking. All along the main street pale faces were pressed to windows. Apparently no one had ever told the citizens of Sawtooth that in many gunfights more innocent bystanders were killed than gunmen.

Fargo looked at the batwing doors. Tucker, he reasoned, must be figuring he would enter through the front, and would greet him with a hail of lead. But not if the same trick worked twice. Turning, he ran to a window halfway to the rear. It was so dirty he couldn't see inside. By the same token, they couldn't see out. He cast about and spotted a small pile of cord wood for a stove against the wall of the next structure. Grabbing the top log, he threw it at the glass and spun and ran the instant the log left his hand. He heard the window break but did not look back. Rounding the front corner, he sprinted four steps to the doors and flung himself through.

The ruse worked like a charm. Three gunmen were looking at the shattered window, not where they should be. Fargo's first shot dropped one dead where the man stood. Thumbing the hammer, he whirled, then stroked the trigger. Another gunman was knocked into the bar, falling amid a shower of glasses. The last man, at the rear, spun to flee, snapping off a wild shot. Fargo aimed at the killer's head, and just as the man reached the hall, he fired.

In the sudden silence that followed, Fargo could hear a clock ticking behind the bar. He dropped low to reload, listening for footsteps, for Tucker's voice, anything. Sawtooth was unaccountably quiet, but not for long. The thud of hooves sounded to the east, echoing along the deserted street like the echoes in a canyon.

Fargo stood and stepped to the entrance. None of the bodies dotting the street moved. He saw a small dog appear further down and trot along as if nothing out of the ordinary were taking place. No riflemen appeared on the buildings, no gunmen at any of the alleys. He eased outside, tilting his hat brim back so it wouldn't block his view of the roofs. Moving to the corner closest to the Ovaro, he stopped and waited for the opposition to show its hand.

Nothing happened. A minute went by, and Fargo moved to the outer edge of the walk. He leaned out from under the overhang to see if he would draw fire. The only sound was the distant wail of a baby.

Fargo took a chance and ran to the pinto. In a smooth swing he was in the saddle and wheeling down the street. He hugged the horn, seeking gunmen in every shadow. None sought to bar his way. He flashed past the hardware store, where the owner shook a fist at him, then past the hotel, where the desk clerk was staggering outside, and soon was past the last building. Only when he was in the clear did he holster the Colt.

At the mouth of the gully Fargo checked for tracks other than those of the Ovaro and the chestnut and was reassured to find none. He started up the gully, then rose in the stirrups, his gaze fastened on a slender form wriggling along in the dirt like an oversize redheaded rattler.

Fargo trotted to her side. "Some people never learn," he said, dismounting. Cassandra growled and tried to go faster, but he plucked her off the ground and held her in both arms while walking up the gully to her horse. She was scraped and torn from extricating herself from the cleft, her once flawless face marred by scratches and grime. He set her down with her back to a large rock, removed the gag, and untied her ankles.

Cassandra coughed, then wet her lips and studied him. "Something went wrong, didn't it, big man? I can tell by your face." She glanced toward the road. "Where's the woman? I thought you were bringing her back?"

Fargo sat on a flat rock and tiredly rubbed his chin. "Who is Wes Tucker?"

"So that's it!" Cassandra responded gleefully. "He got the better of you. What happened? Did he get to the woman first?"

"Who is he?" Fargo pried. "How does he fit into the scheme of things?"

"Wouldn't you like to know!" she rejoined. "I'll never tell, you bastard. And I hope he puts you six feet under before this is done."

Too weary to argue, Fargo reflected on the next step to take. So far all he had succeeded in doing was burning the outlaw sanctuary to the ground and making off with the sister of the two notorious killers, whom he had yet to run into. He had no idea who Tucker was, no idea how to get Lorraine back. Or did he?

Fargo stood, reviewing the events in Sawtooth. If Tucker was connected to the Jefferses, why had Red and the other two gunmen been watching the hotel for Lorraine when they must have known Tucker had gotten to her? Was it because the three had arrived in the middle of the night and by then Lorraine was already in Tucker's clutches? Or was he wrong altogether? Could it be Red and the others hadn't been waiting for Lorraine at all, but had been waiting for *him*? It would explain a lot.

Fargo suddenly walked to Cassandra and set her on the chestnut. He clasped the lariat, then forked leather. At a canter, he rode to within twenty yards of the road and drew rein.

Now that Fargo had time to think, he knew that all the gunmen in town, with the exception of Red and the two from the ranch, had been complete strangers. He'd had a good look at all of Cassandra's leather-slappers during the fight in the house, and not one had been present. So the men in town had been Tucker's, or else had been recruited by Tucker from Sawtooth's rougher element. If he was right, Reece and the rest had yet to arrive. If so, he had a slim hope of rescuing Lorraine.

Fargo saw a single rider go by, an older man who did not look up the gully. Later a wagon clattered past, a canvas spread over the bed. Cassandra fidgeted a lot but made no attempt to flee.

In under half an hour Fargo heard the welcome racket of a large group of horsemen approaching from the southwest. He pulled out the Sharps and rode to within earshot of the road. Shifting, he tugged on the lariat to pull the chestnut up beside the Ovaro. He cocked the rifle, then touched the barrel to the redhead's temple.

Cassandra drew back, her eyes like half-dollars, fear flaring in their depths.

The riders came closer, a pall of dust marking their progress. Fargo saw the heavy gunman leading five tough customers he remembered from the bunkhouse, all so intent on reaching town not one glanced up the gully. He put his left hand to his mouth and yelled, "Reece! Over here!"

In a body the startled killers came to a halt. Several stabbed at their six-shooters but froze at a command from Reece, who then held his pudgy hands out from his sides to show he was not inclined to meet his Maker, and slowly advanced. He stared at Cassandra as if he could not believe his eyes. On reining up, he said, "You have sand, mister. I'll give you that. But when Frank and Bob hear of this, I wouldn't care to be in your boots."

"I'm looking forward to meeting them," Fargo said.

Reece nodded at the Sharps. "What's the meaning of this? You think that you can get us to throw down our hardware by threatening her?"

"No, I want you to deliver a message."

"To her brothers?"

"To Wes Tucker," Fargo said.

"But he—" Reece began, and stopped when Cassandra shook her head.

"He what?" Fargo prompted.

"Nothing. What's the message?"

"I want to arrange a swap. Cassandra Jeffers for Lorraine Knobel."

"Who?"

"The woman I was with at the hotel."

"Her name is Lewis, ain't it?"

"No."

Cassandra was not one to keep silent for long, even with a gun pointed at her head. "And this bastard isn't her husband, either, you lummox. Tell my brothers he's Skye Fargo."

"Fargo? Ain't he the one—"

Again Cassandra interrupted, biting out, "You've said more than enough already! Just go find them and let them know who they're up against. Warn them to be careful. He's slippery as an eel."

Reece nodded and lifted his reins.

"Aren't you forgetting something?" Fargo asked.

"I am?"

"We can't set up a swap unless we agree where to meet. Tell Tucker that I want you to come alone to this exact spot at the same time tomorrow. Have him tell you where he wants to exchange the women. And if he tries any tricks, no one will set eyes on Miss Jeffers again."

Reece nodded. "I'll pass on the word, don't you worry." He smiled at the redhead, then turned and rejoined his men. They lost no time galloping toward Sawtooth, and the moment they were out of sight Fargo gripped the rope firmly and led the chestnut toward town almost as fast.

"What the hell are you up to?" Cassandra wondered. "It won't do you any good to follow them into Sawtooth. If anyone sees me tied up like this, the townspeople themselves will string you up from the nearest tree."

Fargo had no intention of explaining his plan. He cut off the road a quarter of a mile from the first building and rode northward around Sawtooth until he found a vantage point from which he could see the road leading into town at both ends. Positioning the two horses shoulder to shoulder, he stuck the Sharps in the scabbard and reached up to stick the gag in Cassandra's mouth. She snapped at his fingers, tearing off a patch of skin, and when he drew his hands back, she swung one leg over the back of the chestnut and slid to the ground. Like a roadrunner, she was off.

Fargo lashed his reins, overhauling her in moments. Bending, he sank his fingers into her flying mane of hair and yanked, nearly jerking her off her feet. She squealed and kicked, tossing violently in order to break loose, but he held on, slowed the pinto, then jumped down. Cassandra vented a shrewish snarl and tried to bust his knee with a well-placed kick. Fargo twisted and seized her ankle, snapped her leg upward and unbalanced her. She landed with a thump.

"Damn you!" Cassandra cried. "I've never wanted anyone dead as badly as I do you!"

Fargo tried to stick the hankderchief back in. She was having none of it and tried to bite his palm. "Your choice," Fargo said. "Either we do this without you acting up, or so help me I'll hit you so hard you won't be able to talk for a month."

Cassandra was curling her lips to snap again. She slowly relaxed, her mouth twitching with suppressed fury. "You're no gentleman!" she spat.

"Makes us even," Fargo responded. "You're no lady." He applied the gag, roughly lifted her to her feet, and guided her to the horses. This time after he boosted her up he cut off a length of rope and lashed her ankles together under the chestnut. "Now let's see you pull that stunt," he said.

Fargo faced Sawtooth and waited. He knew Tucker had fled after the gunfight, and he had a hunch it would not take Reece long to learn where Tucker had gone, or at least the direction Tucker had taken. He was proven right when a group of riders headed out of town to the east.

Fargo adjusted his cinch for the hard ride ahead and mounted. He saw understanding dawn on Cassandra's face as he pulled on the rope, heading toward the road. By slanting to the left, he came out on it so close behind the gunmen that some of the dust of their passage still hung in the air. He followed, but at a safe distance.

Reece stayed on the road for the next ten miles. At a fork where a narrow trail bisected it, the gunmen bore to the northeast toward densely wooded country. Fargo thought he spied the shimmering surface of a lake among the trees higher up but couldn't be sure until he had gone another four miles. He was able to gauge how close he was to Tucker by how upset Cassandra became. She fidgeted more and more, desperate to warn her men.

A squat tableland reared before them. Fargo paralleled the trail rather than riding on it. The risk of being found out was too great. He stopped frequently to survey the landscape, and it was during one of these stops that he heard the clang of metal on metal. It was repeated, in steady cadence, as if someone was hard at work with a hammer.

Fargo rode a hundred feet more, then climbed down and tied both horses. He had learned not to put anything past Cassandra, and since he didn't want her alerting the men ahead, he untied her legs, hauled her off the chestnut, and with a firm grip on her arm, grabbed the Sharps and advanced.

The pines were thick, the brush heavy in spots. He had no difficulty sneaking to within ten yards of a clear strip bordering the south side of the small lake. Revealed before him was a rustic camp consisting of a single large log cabin that looked as if it had been constructed by a drunk, several lean-tos, a rickety corral, and an equally pathetic shed. Horses filled the corral and were tied to a makeshift hitching post at the cabin. Eight gunmen lounged about, talking and smoking. Near the shed a brawny man stripped to the waist pounded on a horseshoe.

Fargo was more interested in the cabin. Neither of the windows had glass or were covered by curtains. He could see men moving around every so often, but no sign of Lorraine. Shoving Cassandra onto her back, he straddled her legs and hunkered down to await developments.

They were not long in coming. None other that Wes Tucker appeared, strolling from the cabin with Reece. The two walked to the corral, deep in discussion. Tucker then barked out names and five gunmen hustled over. He issued instructions, but what they were Fargo couldn't hear over the clanging of the hammer. The five men shortly mounted and rode off toward town.

Fargo was glad to see them go. They were five less he had to worry about when he went in after Lorraine. He hoped more would leave before evening came, but none did.

About four in the afternoon, as Fargo was stifling a yawn after so many hours without sleep, he saw two men take rifles from their saddle scabbards and head toward the woods. It all happened so fast, they were heading in his general direction before he realized their intent. Dropping onto his stomach on top of Cassandra, he held the Sharps in front of him, his thumb on the hammer.

Cassandra had dozed throughout the day. Now, as his added weight pressed down on her, she awakened with a start and stared at him in confusion. She tried shifting but he held her motionless, since the slightest noise might give them away.

The gunmen entered the forest, their boots crunching twigs underfoot. Fargo guessed they were going after game for the supper pot. They would pass within five or six feet of his hiding place, much too close for comfort. Their low voices grew louder.

"—want to be the jackass who took her. Those three will skin him alive and cut out his tongue and eyes, and that's just for starters."

"I'll be glad when Frank and Bob get here. The older one is too damned sour all the time. He never has a good word for anyone."

"Don't let him hear you say that. He'll shoot you for the hell of it."

Fargo, peering through the brush at ground level, saw their legs moving steadily nearer. He glanced up but could not as yet see their faces.

"Sometimes I wonder why the hell I stay on. Why any of us do."

"I'll give you two reasons: The money is good, and we're all wanted elsewhere. Sawtooth is the only town we can go into without having to look over our shoulders every minute of the day. We'd be fools to leave."

"I reckon so. But it sure would be nice if we didn't have to abide that moody buzzard."

Fargo saw them clearly as they crossed an open space. They

126

would have seen him, too, had they not been looking at one another. They went around a pine, moving off to the northwest. Cassandra suddenly bucked and tried moving her legs to draw their attention, but he pinned her down.

"At least he's spending most of his time with that Lewis gal, and not picking on us," one of them remarked.

"She's a spirited filly. Did you see how she stood up to him? Too bad she's not long for this world. Once Les and the boys bring back Fargo's carcass, that grouch Homer will finish her off."

"After he has his fun. He . . ."

The voices trailed away. Fargo slid off Cassandra and rose to his knees. He was glad to learn Lorraine was indeed in the cabin. And now he knew where the five riders had gone earlier—to dispose of him. He also had gleaned another important piece of information, and to test whether it was true or not, he glanced down at the firebrand. "So the man who goes around calling himself Wes Tucker is really named Homer. Homer Jeffers. Now everything fits together."

Cassandra tried to hold her features still to show no reaction, but her expressive eyes betrayed the truth.

"Homer was the one who tried to have the murders blamed on me in order to stop me from tracking down Frank and Bob," Fargo whispered. "He was the one who really killed those four people. And since he must figure that I know, he's not about to let me ride off with Lorraine so I can turn him in to the law. He'll do whatever it takes to rub me out."

The expression on Cassandra's face showed that she would dearly love to do the same.

"Your family has had a sweet deal here," Fargo remarked quietly. "You run a town that's in business mainly to give killers, robbers, and others a place to lie low. You probably get a percentage of the saloon profits and whatever else you can dip into. And since you wanted to keep out of sight yourselves, you had the ranch built, and this place. And there must be more." He paused. "The Jeffers empire is about to come to an end."

Cassandra raised a leg to kick him and Fargo slammed her flat. "Not a peep," he growled in her ear, then hoisted her erect and hurried to the horses. He bound her securely, tying her to a tree so she couldn't crawl off again. "I have a score to settle with your brothers," he said before he moved off. "But I'm going to save you to turn over to the sheriff in Kingfish. I don't know if they can peg any crimes on you, but I'm hoping they can. It would serve you right to spend the rest of your days behind bars."

Fargo claimed the Sharps and headed toward the south side of the lake. He made sure he had a round in the chamber of the Sharps. So far the Jefferses had pretty much had their way, keeping him on the run most of the time. Now he was going to take the fight to them, in earnest.

12

The south shore of the small lake was dense with mountain hawthorne that grew close to the rear corner of the cabin. Fargo stealthily stalked to the last bushy tree and squatted there until the sun dipped below the horizon and the light from a lantern spilled out the front windows. Five gunmen remained, counting Homer Jeffers and Reece, who spent most of the time indoors.

Fargo watched the three men at the fire. After one of them turned in early and the other two became involved in a friendly card game using sticks as chips, he crawled toward the rear wall. He had to freeze when one of the players idly glanced at the cabin. The gunman never noticed him and went back to dealing a hand. Creeping forward, Fargo reached the base of the wall and discovered thin gaps that permitted him to hear what was being said inside. At that moment, Reece was speaking.

"—ain't saying that we ought to cut and run, Homer. I'm just pointing out that this Fargo is more dangerous than most we've tangled with. You should have seen him at the house, when we were pounding on him something awful. The man never showed a lick of fear. He fought back until he couldn't fight anymore."

"He's flesh and blood, like you and me," Homer Jeffers said. "A few lead pills or six inches of cold steel will get him out of our hair for good."

"If we can catch him," Reece said, and he did not sound very confident.

"You worry me, Otis," Homer said. "I never took you for yellow or a quitter."

"You know better!" Reece countered. "I'm not no fool, either. I wouldn't take a rabid wolf lightly, and this hellion in buckskins is worse than any rabid wolf. You saw what he did in town. Hell, if he was to offer his gun for hire, he'd be the highest paid son of a bitch in all of Texas."

"Frank and Bob are both better than this Fargo," Homer said. "We have nothing to worry about."

"I suppose." There was a lengthy pause. "What about the woman here? I don't like keeping her alive. She knows too damn much."

"She lives until my sister is safe. Then I'll do to her the same as I did to the family dog when I was seven or eight. Lord, you should have heard him howl when I peeled his skin off!"

Fargo had heard enough. He stepped to the far corner, and from there to the front. One of the horses in the corral nickered, but the cardplayers paid no heed and went on playing. Bending, Fargo darted to the lake side of the enclosure and around it to the gate. A single rail sufficed to pen the horses in. In moments he had eased it to the grass.

A few of the horses paced back and forth, sensing something out of the ordinary was taking place. Fargo made for the lake again. A roan suddenly whinnied loudly, which brought both the poker players and the sleeping man to their feet.

"What's with the stock?" one said.

"Must have smelled a wildcat or bear," answered another.

Crouched by the water's edge, Fargo lowered his mouth close to the ground so the gunmen wouldn't be able to pinpoint his position and gave voice to his best imitation of a snarling mountain lion. Years of wilderness living had given him an uncanny knack for imitating a variety of wild beasts, and there were old-timers who swore his calls were so authentic he'd fool the real article. His snarl fooled the horses, which milled in panic a few short seconds and then bolted for the open gate.

"Damn!" a gunman bellowed. "Catch them!"

"Reece! Homer! The horses are running off!" wailed the man who had tried to catch some sleep.

The three gunmen raced after the fleeing animals as Fargo

raced to the cabin, going around to the opposite side in time to see Homer and Reece join the mad dash after the mounts. Horses and outlaws plunged into the woods. Instantly Fargo dashed inside.

Lorraine Knobel, gagged and tied hand and foot, was slumped in a corner, her face streaked with dirt. Small drops of blood dotted her neck, arms, and legs as high as her knees. She saw him and tried to sit up, tears rimming her eyes.

"Hang on," Fargo said, rushing over. He set down the Sharps, yanked out the filthy cloth jammed in her mouth, and drew the toothpick to cut the ropes. Her gasp made him spin around.

Otis Reece stood framed in the doorway, a Colt in his right hand. Fargo's own Colt. "Good thing I looked back when I did," he said, grinning. "Homer will pay me a hefty bonus for this." He advanced a ponderous stride. "Lift your hands real slow and step away from your cannon."

Fargo acted as if he were going to comply. His right hand was next to his right boot, holding the toothpick. As he rose, he began to elevate his arms, keeping his right arm close to his chest so Reece couldn't see the throwing knife.

"That's it," the stout gunman said. "Nice and slow."

"Just go easy on that trigger," Fargo said. And in a twinkling he sprang to the left and whirled, hurling the toothpick with pinpoint accuracy, aiming for Reece's heart. He would have slain the gunman, too, had Reece not snapped his arm higher to shoot and caught the blade in the forearm instead of the chest. Reece yelped, the Colt banged into the wall, and Fargo leaped, landing a blow that would have knocked down most men but only rocked Reece on his heels. Reece tried to bring the Colt to bear and Fargo struck him twice on the jaw, causing Reece to totter and lose his grip on the pistol.

Fargo tried to snatch the revolver, but Reece recovered and caught hold of his shirt with one hand while flinging back the other to strike. Fargo brought his left arm up, blocking the blow. Infuriated, Reece intentionally flung himself at the floor, trying to pin Fargo under his great bulk. Fargo shifted, dived, and was able to roll out from under before they smashed down. He scrambled to his feet and felt his ankle gripped.

"Gonna kill you, bastard!" Reece rumbled, and brutally yanked. Fargo's foot swept out from under him. He fell next to the gunman, who tore the toothpick out and sheared it at his face. Fargo jerked backward in the nick of time. The blade imbedded itself in the plank near his ear.

Reece heaved to his knees, slashing wildly. Fargo leaped to the left and collided with a small table he hadn't even known was there. Down he went, to his hands and knees, as Reece charged. He flipped backward to evade the toothpick, bumped the table again, and leaped up and over. For a moment they were in a stalemate, Reece on one side, Fargo on the other.

"You're not so tough, after all," the gunman cracked.

"Is that so, quitter?" Fargo replied, trying to provoke the other man. He succeeded. Reece drove the knife at his chest but was unable to get close with the table there. Fargo skipped to the right, swinging around the end and going for the pistol at his hip. He had Reece dead to rights. Or would have, had the fat man not kicked the table, sending it crashing into Fargo's legs.

Fargo went down, the revolver skidding off. Reece was on him before he could rise, a boot the size of a club hitting him in the side. He hit the wall, pain racking his chest. Getting a hand under him, he tried to stand. He was only partway up when Reece came at him again.

The bloody toothpick descended. Fargo ducked and the blade nicked his hat. He moved to the right again, staying just ahead of more vicious swings. Then he spotted his own Colt, lying a yard away. He threw himself at it as if he was diving into water, his right hand closing on the smooth grips as Reece closed in. Shoving onto his back, he thumbed back the hammer and fired just as Reece stabbed, fired again as Reece staggered and raised the toothpick, and then fired a third and final time as the knife swooped toward him. Reece melted to the floor, his thick lips working soundlessly.

Fargo quickly stood, shoving his Colt where it belonged. The toothpick was at his feet. He snatched it up and ran to Lorraine to cut her loose.

"Skye!" she said. "I thought I was a goner until you came in that door! The one who reeks like a polecat kept jabbing me with his pocketknife and telling me all the horrible things he was going to do to me once you were taken care of."

"If we don't get out here, he might have the chance," Fargo cautioned, slicing rapidly. He freed her wrists first, then her legs, and helped her to her feet. The Arkansas toothpick went back in the sheath. He knew he should reload the Colt, but there might not be time—not when Homer Jeffers and the others were bound to have heard the shots and were rushing back. Taking the rifle, he grasped her hand and darted to the doorway.

Figures flitted through the trees, converging on the cabin. "Look there!" a man shouted. "Who the hell is that?"

"It's Fargo," Homer roared. "Blow out his lamp!"

Pistols spat flame and lead. Fargo ran out and to the right, pulling Lorraine in his wake. Slugs tore into the cabin on either side of them. Lorraine cried out but did not fall. He cleared the corner and so did she, and for the moment they were in the clear.

Fargo flew between the corral and the water, then veered around the shed and paused to look back. The killers were at the corner of the cabin, scouring the night for them. Evidently one of their shots had torn through the cabin wall and struck the lantern. Flames danced in the windows, licking upward.

Lorraine had doubled over and was breathing loudly. Out of fear, Fargo thought. He draped an arm over her shoulder and steered her toward the woods in nimble-footed haste.

"There they are!" someone shouted.

Shots rent the night. Bullets slammed into the shed, into the ground around them.

Fargo reached the tree line and swung Lorraine behind a pine. Lead smacked the trunk close to his head. Whirling, he saw that one of the gunmen had climbed the rails of the corral and was firing from there. Fargo brought up the Sharps, aimed at the center of the killer's dark outline, and fired.

The gunman was hurled rearward, arms and legs flailing the air.

Seizing Lorraine's wrist, Fargo ran flat out. The Sharps was empty, the Colt might be. He needed distance, needed time to reload. Above and around them bullets clipped off leaves, chipped off bark, bit into the earth. Fewer shots came close, though, as they penetrated deeper. The shouts of the outlaws gradually faded.

Fargo figured they had gone three quarters of a mile before it was safe to halt so they could catch their breath. He released Lorraine so she could sit if she wanted and was surprised to see she was still bent over. "City life does it every time," he joked to ease her anxiety.

"I'm hit."

Fargo took her in his arms and eased her down next to a trunk. "Where?" he asked, and as he did, he felt a warm, sticky sensation on his right hand.

"My side," Lorraine said, giving a little shiver. "But don't fret. I can keep going."

"I should examine you," Fargo said.

"Not until we're safe. I won't let myself fall into their clutches again! That terrible man would do vile things to me, things I can't bear to think about!" She clutched his wrist. "He bragged about murdering my parents. Said he laughed in my mother's face as she pleaded for her life. Please, Skye! Get me the hell out of here!"

Fargo nodded and took her hand. Hiking westward, stopping frequently, they circled around to where the horses were tied. He was half worried Cassandra would be gone, but she was right where he had left her—for once.

"Who is this?" Lorraine asked.

"Homer's sister."

"Are the ropes necessary? Is she just like him?"

"Worse."

"That's not possible."

Fargo gave Lorraine a boost onto the chestnut, then placed the redhead over the back of the Ovaro. Cassandra stubbornly resisted but could inflict little harm, bound as she was. He stepped into the stirrups, and as he turned to go he saw the blazing cabin through the trees. The structure was completely engulfed. Chuckling, he gave Cassandra a pat on her backside. "If I keep this up, your family won't have anyplace left to hang their hats."

Fortunately the gag garbled her response.

Fargo rode to the northwest, staying well clear of the trail. From the lay of the land, he suspected the lake fed into streams, and he hoped to find one before too long. The darkness and the ever-present threat of the killers forced him to go much slower than he liked. He saw Lorraine slumped over and rode alongside her in case she became too weak to go on. This latest wound, coming as it did so soon after her head injury, might leave her too weak to ride and in dire need of a doctor.

The gentle gurgling of water perked up Fargo's hopes. He homed in on the sound and soon reined up next to a shallow stream. Lorraine tried to dismount on her own and would have fallen had he not been there to catch her. He heard Cassandra laugh and wished to high heaven she wasn't a woman so he could break every bone in her body with a clear conscience.

In a tiny hollow shielded by pines Fargo started a small fire. He stripped his saddle and bedroll off the Ovaro and prepared a bed for Lorraine. Blood had formed a wide ring above her waist. She sank back weakly, smiling as he hovered over her.

"Never realized you were such a mother hen."

Fargo brought water in his tin cup, then had her open her dress. Her undergarments were also soaked. Lifting a burning brand on high to give more light, he carefully inspected the wound. It turned out the bullet had only grazed her, digging a furrow an inch deep below her last rib. Her vital organs had been spared.

Fargo tossed the brand into the fire and walked to the Ovaro. He lowered Cassandra to the grass, hitched the hem of her dress, and tore off a swath. This he dipped in the stream and used to thoroughly clean the furrow. The hours of torment and lack of food and sleep caught up with Lorraine. She passed out before he was done.

Against his better judgment, Fargo removed the redhead's gag and hauled a log closer to the fire for her to prop herself against. She was strangely quiet as he brought her water and a small piece of jerky from his saddlebags. She accepted the morsel without complaint and did not try to bite off his fingers. "I'll give you more in the morning," he said.

"I'm going to kill her, you know."

Fargo was rising to get more rope. "What?"

Cassandra nodded at the unconscious Lorraine. "One way or the other, I'll see that she joins her beloved ma and pa before this is done."

"You're insane."

"Think so?" Cassandra giggled. "Mister, you're hardly a fit judge. How many have you killed in your time? Judging by what I've seen, I'd say more than a handful. If we were to compare notches, you'd have me beat by a long shot."

"I don't murder people in cold blood."

The redhead shrugged. "Does that really make a difference? Killing is killing, no matter how you look at it. Folks have put a brand on my brothers because they're so good at it, but they're no different than those who wear a badge and kill for a living in the name of the law."

"You truly believe that?" Fargo said, sadly shaking his head. Where before she had disgusted him, he now almost felt sorry for her. She wasn't wicked, as such. She was simply three shoes shy of the four needed to have a pony plated.

"Don't look at me like that!" Cassandra said. "I don't want your pity. I can look out for myself. As you'll find out soon enough."

Fargo tied her to the log but did not put the handkerchief back in her mouth. "I won't gag you if you don't act up," he said.

"Don't do me any favors, big man. It's too late to start treating me nice. If I get the chance, I'll scratch out your eyes."

Deciding not to waste any more breath on her, Fargo lay down beside Lorraine, even though he knew he should stay awake all night, standing watch. But he had been so long without sleep that if he failed to get a few hours of rest, he would be worthless come morning. He closed his eyes and put his hands on his chest and was just drifting off when he had the sort of feeling that came over him when he was riding through Indian country and sensed hostiles watching him. He looked around and saw Cassandra Jeffers staring at him, simply sitting and staring without batting an eyelash, the hatred she radiated like a physical force. She gave him a sinister smile, which was all the more chilling in the harsh glare of the fire. To gall her, he grinned and winked, then pulled his hat brim low and went to sleep.

Shortly before daybreak, Fargo awoke. He automatically sat up and surveyed the area. Right away he noticed Cassandra still staring balefully at him, and he wondered if she had been doing it the whole night through. "Morning," he said.

"Another day, another opportunity to rip out your innards."

"Still have your sweet disposition, I see," Fargo remarked as he turned to Lorraine. She had stirred and now awakened. "How do you feel?"

"Refreshed," Lorraine answered, sitting. She gritted her teeth and gingerly touched her side. "I hurt terribly, but I don't feel nearly as weak as I did last night."

"Good. Then we can head out at sunrise."

"Where to?"

"Ripclaw," Fargo said.

"Why there? Why not Kingfish?"

"From where we are, Ripclaw is closer. And we have to get you to safety as fast as we can. The town marshal won't be any too happy to see me, but he won't blow my head off once he's talked to you."

Cassandra had to throw in her opinion. "Why lie to her, handsome? Why get her hopes up when you know damn well you'll never see Ripclaw or any other town again?" She sneered at Lorraine. "You're dead, honey, and you just don't know it. By now my brother Homer has reached Sawtooth. He's probably offered a king's ransom to the man who will bring him your protector's head. A small army is out right this minute scouring the countryside for us. We won't get ten miles."

Lorraine glanced at Skye. "Do you think she's right?"

"Maybe. It doesn't matter if she is," Fargo said. "We can't stay here. And we can't hide out until Homer tires of looking for us. You need a doctor. Wounds like yours can become infected, even if we do our best to keep it clean. We won't take the risk."

"How touching!" Cassandra said in disgust.

Fargo marched over to her and she cowered back. Squatting, he gripped the bottom of her dress and tore off another swath, then moistened the material. "Open your dress," he told Lorraine. After she did, he bandaged her. "I have a little jerky left," he mentioned. "It will have to do for breakfast. We have no idea how close Homer and his boys are, so I can't shoot any game."

"I'm so starved it doesn't matter," Lorraine said. "Jerky will be fine."

"Jerky will be fine!" Cassandra mimicked her. "Lord, I can't wait to be shed of the two of you."

"We can leave you here if you want," Fargo said.

"In the middle of nowhere? I doubt you have it in you. You're tougher than any man I've ever run across, but you're just like all the rest in one respect." Cassandra lowered her voice as if confiding a secret. "You have a soft spot, mister. As you pointed out, you're not a cold-blooded killer. You won't go off and leave me here, knowing I might be found by wild animals or Comanches."

Fargo disliked having her see right through him. He put on a stern face and bent over her. "You could be wrong. Keep prodding and you'll find out." She had no retort to that, so he saddled the Ovaro and doused the fire.

Due west seemed to Fargo to be the safest route. He took the precaution of gagging the redhead first, to keep her from calling out should they spy searchers from Sawtooth. To his surprise, she didn't put up a fight. She seemed eager to be off, perhaps in the belief they would soon be caught.

There was no established trail, so Fargo picked the path of least resistance as he went along, mindful to always stay under cover. All went well for the first hour, and then they came to the rim of the tableland and were confronted by a sheer slope much too treacherous for the horses. "We'll have to find another way down," Fargo said to Lorraine, bearing northward. He soon discovered a few game trails, none wide enough for their mounts.

Fargo was beginning to wonder if the trail he had taken up to the lake was the only one when the steep slope was replaced by a low, winding wash that would take them to the flatland below. He went over the edge, watching alertly as the pinto picked its way with instinctive care. The Ovaro was doubly burdened, what with Cassandra seated behind him, and had to go slowly. He had toyed with the notion of slinging her on the horse on her belly, but had relented since she had been behaving herself.

A small switchback took the stallion toward the bottom. Fargo sat relaxed but wary, so intent on not having a spill that he hardly noticed when Cassandra Jeffers shifted her weight a little. The Ovaro went around the bend. As it did, Fargo twisted to check on Lorraine. The instant he turned, Cassandra drove her right shoulder into his back with all her strength, and before he could catch hold of anything, he was knocked from the saddle and sent tumbling down the slope. Above him the redhead cackled. He struck a boulder and lay there, stunned, unable to lift a finger as Cassandra Jeffers slid over the cantle onto the saddle, jabbed her knees into the pinto, and made her bid to escape.

13

Skye Fargo knew he must stop the redhead at all costs. He resisted the icy grip of darkness enfolding his mind and rolled onto his side. Cassandra was on the lower half of the switchback, ten yards from the bottom of the wash and half that distance from where he lay. Girding his arms, he managed to rise on one knee. She was almost abreast of him. Fargo dug his boot heels into the loose soil to gain purchase and leaped, trying to snare the Ovaro's reins. His fingertips missed by a fraction and he tumbled lower.

Cassandra chortled with glee.

From up the slope came a furious, "No!" Fargo looked and saw Lorraine Knobel galloping down the switchback, her long, dark hair flying. She handled the chestnut like an expert, streaking around the bend without slowing.

Fargo doubted she could overtake Cassandra. Once the Ovaro reached level ground it would outrun the chestnut in no time. He had to slow the redhead down. To that end, he lurched erect, took two long, vaulting strides, and jumped for all he was worth. He landed short of the bottom and jumped again, throwing himself in the stallion's path. Cassandra tried to run him down, jabbing her heels to spur the pinto on, but the pinto slid to a stop and half reared, its front hooves sweeping upward. Cassandra tried to swing around but she had a hard time guiding the Ovaro using just her legs. Fargo made a grab for the bridle and narrowly missed.

All this time, Lorraine had been hastening to his aid. She clattered down the last part of the switchback just as Cassandra succeeded in skirting Fargo. Cassandra pumped her feet to bring the pinto to a gallop. She was hampered by being unable to use her hands, and she looked back in dismay as the chestnut drew within arm's reach.

Fargo thought that Lorraine would seize hold of the Ovaro. To his amazement, she dived off her horse and slammed into Cassandra Jeffers. They fell, locked together, Cassandra striving to butt Lorraine with her forehead. Fargo ran to help, but Lorraine needed none. She cuffed Cassandra, then held Jeffers down.

"You're not going anywhere, bitch!"

Cassandra heaved and fought in vain. She arced a knee at Lorraine's spine but Lorraine was too smart for her and shifted aside.

Fargo ran up and gripped the redhead by the shoulders. As Lorraine slid off, he dragged Cassandra, kicking every step of the way, to the Ovaro. Never again would he give her the benefit of the doubt. He lashed her ankles and heaved her over the back of the Ovaro, facedown.

"That was close," Lorraine said, brushing dirt from her dress.

"You did fine," Fargo complimented her, and she blushed. "How's your side?"

"It hurts worse than ever, but it was worth it to give that woman a taste of her own medicine."

A little the worse for wear, they remounted, and Fargo assumed the lead, riding due west. Until noon they moved through brushy country, where they could stay hidden most of the time. Past the brush was arid, open land broken by gullies, jumbled boulders, and box canyons.

Fargo drew rein at the edge of the chaparral and scanned for movement or telltale dust clouds. The land ahead appeared as barren as the lifeless soil. He concentrated on the country to the south, toward Sawtooth.

"There's no one," Lorraine commented, also surveying the land before them.

"Keep your eyes peeled. If they catch us in the open, they can pick us off from a distance."

"Let's wait until dark."

"I wish we could," Fargo said, riding from concealment. He yanked the Sharps out and adjusted the sight for maximum

141

range. Should they be spotted, the Sharps was all that would stand between life and death.

The sun was hotter, the air likewise. Fargo loosened his bandanna and offered it to Lorraine, who accepted gratefully and used it to tie up her long hair. Cassandra was back to her old trick of glaring at him without letup. He ignored her completely.

Two more hours went by without incident. Fargo was nearing a narrow canyon when Lorraine yelled sharply.

"Dust! There!"

It was a huge dust cloud to the southeast, and it was sweeping in their direction. As yet, Fargo couldn't distinguish the riders, which meant the riders had yet to see them. "We have to take cover," he said. He urged the Ovaro into the canyon, but only went a short distance. Dismounting, he handed Lorraine the reins. "Stay here and watch our friend."

Racing to a man-sized boulder at the canyon mouth, Fargo crouched. The dust cloud expanded, opening to reveal nine gunmen. At the head rode Homer Jeffers, beside him an Indian or half-breed in a headband, a tracker scouring the packed earth for prints. They would pass within five hundred yards of the canyon and were bound to notice the fresh trail leading toward it.

Fargo brought the Sharps to bear and aligned the sight with his eye. His first shot would be the most important. If he succeeded, he might end it then and there. He saw the riders trot closer to the tracks, saw the tracker gesture excitedly. The killers reined up and the man in the headband slid down to study the hoofprints. Then the man rose and pointed directly at the canyon.

Homer Jeffers motioned. The gunmen fanned out, some pulling rifles from scabbards.

Fargo aimed at Homer. Jeffers was the key. Slay him and the rest might give up. He set the rear trigger and lightly touched the front trigger, but didn't fire. He wanted Homer well within range. There must be no mistakes—not with so much at stake. Mentally, he ticked off the yardage. The outlaws were four hundred and fifty yards away, then four hundred, and although Fargo had made longer shots, he continued to hold his fire, waiting for the perfect moment—which came at three hundred yards. He had a dead bead on Homer Jeffers, had the man dead to rights, and he slowly curled his finger until the Sharps thundered and bucked against his shoulder.

At that very second, just as Fargo fired, the tracker made the mistake of riding his horse in front of Homer's, his gaze glued to the prints. The .52-caliber slug hit him with the impact of a battering ram, lifting him clean off his mount.

Immediately the killers spread out farther, those with rifles cutting loose. Not one had a Sharps, so their rounds all fell short, spewing tiny geysers of dirt dozens of yards from the boulder.

Fargo did not spend time chiding himself over the miss. It had not been his fault. He compensated, swiveling and sighting on Homer. Again he cocked the hammer, set the trigger. He was a heartbeat from firing when Homer unexpectedly slanted to the north and adopted a Comanche trick. The butcher swung onto the off side of his mount and fired over the saddle.

Fargo shot the horse. The animal crashed to the earth in a whirl of limbs and tail, spilling Homer in a heap. Homer, shaken, tried to rise. Fargo worked the trigger guard, slipped in a new cartridge. He hurried, afraid one of the other gunmen would rescue Jeffers before he could shoot. He swung the Sharps out, rushed aiming, and fired.

Inches from Homer the ground erupted. He frantically scrambled behind his dead horse and snapped off a few shots.

Now Fargo *was* annoyed at himself. He should have taken the two or three extra seconds he would have needed to be absolutely sure. Reloading, he suddenly realized three of the killers were sweeping straight toward him and were only a hundred yards out. He sighted on the first and blew the man out of the saddle. The remaining pair had more courage than common sense. They kept on coming, one blasting with a pistol, the other a rifle. A few bullets whined off the boulder, chipping off bits of stone.

Fargo shot the gunman wielding the rifle. The other tried to flee, but he was much too close. At sixty yards Fargo put a bullet between his shoulder blades and he painted the side of his horse's neck red as he pitched off.

Turning, Fargo sought Homer Jeffers and was angered to see Jeffers riding double with another man, speeding northward. He brought the Sharps up, but they disappeared around a bend in the canyon, as the rest had already done. The gunshots ceased and the hoofbeats faded in the distance.

Standing, Fargo jogged to the horses and swung up without a word. He galloped out of the canyon, riding to the southwest, Lorraine keeping pace beside him. She saw the bodies but made no comment.

Fargo guessed it would take Jeffers five minutes or better to regroup and plot an attack. By the time the butcher realized they were gone, they should have a two- or three-mile lead. He noticed Cassandra was slipping off and reached around to pull her snug against the cantle. She growled and kicked, making him realize she hadn't been slipping off at all. She was deliberately trying to fall, in the hope her brother would soon find her.

The thought spurred Fargo into reining up. He slid down, grasped the back of Cassandra's dress, and swung her to the ground as if she were a sack of grain. She grunted as he propped her against a boulder. "You look a little peaked," he said, giving her head a pat. "The sun will do you good." Cassandra flicked her feet at him and he skipped aside and mounted. "Give my regards to your brother."

Cassandra glared after them. Fargo rubbed salt into her wounded pride by waving cheerily. Then he devoted himself to riding.

"Why did you leave her?" Lorraine asked. "I was looking forward to seeing her put in prison."

"She will be," Fargo pledged. "But she slowed us down too much with all her shenanigans. And she'll buy us a few more minutes when they stop to untie her and hear her story."

"She'll never rest until we're both dead. You know that, don't you?"

"Let her try. I don't make it a habit to shoot women, but in her case I'll make an exception."

"Would you really?"

Something in her voice made Fargo glance around. He was mildly surprised to see how somber she had grown, and he realized that his answer meant a great deal to her. "No," he admitted, "not if I can avoid it."

Her relief was transparent. "Thank you."

Across the burning Texas terrain they fled for the next hour and a half. Fargo did not feel safe in slowing until they came to grassland. He never took his gaze from their back trail for very long, yet the killers never appeared. "I wonder what's holding them up?" he said to himself.

"Are you complaining?" Lorraine laughed, and swatted dust from her sleeve. "Be thankful they haven't shown. My horse is about on its last legs."

The chestnut had given signs of flagging the last few miles and now walked with its head hanging. Fargo studied its legs for evidence the animal was going short, but there was none. In order not to press their luck, he slowed even more. In a while they came to a well-marked trail running from east to west.

"Where does this lead?" Lorraine asked.

"Ripclaw."

"Then we're home free!"

"Not hardly," Fargo said, removing his hat to fan his face. "Homer is a savvy customer. He'll expect us to go this way. Which is why we'll take to open country as soon as it gets dark."

"Do you think we can lose them?"

"We'll try. Unless they have another tracker, we might pull it off," Fargo said. He shoved his hat back on and lifted the reins. That was when he spotted a pair of riders far ahead, riding toward them.

"Oh, look!" Lorraine cried. "Maybe they'll help us."

"Don't get your hopes up. Most folks out here tend to mind their own business. And when they hear who is after us, they might light a shuck for parts unknown."

"You never know."

Fargo rested a hand on the Sharps, to be prepared. He wouldn't put it past Homer Jeffers to have sent gunmen toward Ripclaw earlier, and these might be them returning. After all, by Homer's reckoning he and the women could have reached the trail by morning if they'd ridden through the night. If these were some of the butcher's hired guns, they'd try to get as close as they could before unlimbering their hardware.

Lorraine was fussing with her hair and her dress to make herself presentable.

Fargo eased the Colt a bit looser in his holster. The two riders were now near enough for him to determine that one was in his early twenties, the other pushing thirty. Both had dark hair and both favored two guns, rare among gunmen. The younger man wore a black vest and hat, the other one a black suit that gave him the aspect of an undertaker. Fargo could not say why, but a sudden feeling of great danger welled up inside of him.

The riders came to within thirty yards and then did a strange thing. They left the trail, angling to the right, swinging well wide of Fargo and Lorraine in order to avoid passing them.

"What in the world?" Lorraine wondered.

Fargo was puzzled, too, until a vivid recollection of his visit to Waco told him who they were and why they behaved as they did. He began to lift the Sharps, then thought better of the idea. Lorraine was too vulnerable. She might survive the shoot-out, but if he lost, they'd finish her off. So he merely nodded at them and the older one nodded back, and then the pair had gone on by. Once they were thirty yards to the rear, they swung back onto the trail and continued toward Sawtooth.

"I never saw anyone act so peculiar," Lorraine remarked. "You'd think they'd have the decency to pass the time of day, at least."

"Ride," Fargo said.

"What?"

"Ride faster."

"Whatever for?"

"Just do it!" Fargo said, clucking the Ovaro to a canter, which he held for the next half a mile. Her chestnut was about played out when he dropped to a walk again and twisted to watch the stretch of trail they had just covered.

"What is the matter with you? Did you know them?" Lorraine demanded.

"Never met the gentlemen before."

"If you ask me, this is getting to you."

"In more ways than you know," Fargo said, and was glad when she dropped the subject. He noted the position of the sun in the afternoon sky, wishing it would set sooner than would be the case. A small cluster of trees broke the monotony of the prairie to the southwest and he promptly headed toward them.

"What are you up to now?"

"Saving our hides." Fargo didn't tell her that they were in much greater danger than before, that the odds of them reaching Ripclaw had been drastically reduced. She would learn soon enough if events proved him right. The chestnut faltered a few times, and he had to swat it on the rump to keep it moving. Once they gained the sanctuary of the trees, he climbed down and hid the horses at the far end.

Lorraine collapsed with her back to a tree. "The day isn't over yet and I'm exhausted." She closed her eyes, licked her dry lips. "If it means anything, you were right back at the cemetery. I see now that I never should have come. But I wanted so much to catch the man who murdered my folks, to make him pay with his life, to see him die before my own eyes."

"Even if it was me," Fargo said. He stood where he could see the trail as far back as the horizon. At the moment it was empty.

Lorraine glanced up at him. "You suspected?"

"That you didn't really trust me at first? That you only came along so you could shoot me once you knew for certain I was the one?" Fargo nodded. "It wasn't hard to figure out."

"I'm sorry."

"No need to be. You did what you had to. We all do." Fargo began pacing. He had a feeling that he was making a mistake, that they should press on no matter how worn out the chestnut might be. A tree with low limbs gave him an idea. "I want a better look," he announced, stepping over to it and leaping. He caught hold of a branch and pulled himself higher, climbing with agile skill until the limbs were too thin to support his weight. He could see farther now, perhaps a mile or more, and the sight he beheld sent him flying groundward.

"What's the matter?" Lorraine asked, startled by his abrupt descent.

"Mount up. They're coming."

"Oh, God."

The all-too-brief rest had done little to revitalize the chestnut. It stumbled as Lorraine brought it to a gallop, but recovered and ran gamely on.

Fargo continued to the southwest. The trees would keep the killers from spotting them for a while, and by then he wanted to be well out of sight of the trail. It all depended on whether the chestnut held up. The Ovaro was too tired to bear both of them very far, very fast.

The group of riders Fargo had seen from the tree had been bigger than he expected. He reviewed the fight at the canyon, accounting for four of the nine outlaws in the bunch. That left five, including Homer. Fargo added Cassandra and the two men encountered earlier, making a grand total of eight hardened cutthroats who would stop at nothing to see them dead.

For the next quarter of an hour Fargo and Lorraine sped across the rolling plain. All went well until they came to a grassy basin and headed down the gentle slope. The chestnut let out a whinny, then suddenly buckled, pitching into a roll. Lorraine cried out and barely managed to leap clear in time.

Cursing, Fargo reined up as the chestnut flipped completely over and slid some ten feet. He was off the Ovaro before the chestnut stopped moving, running first to Lorraine, who nodded and smiled wanly while rising to show she was all right, and then to the chestnut, which lay wheezing and nickering pitiably. Fargo felt its legs and could find no broken bones. The horse was simply too exhausted to so much as stand.

"What now?" Lorraine asked at his elbow.

"We keep going."

"They'll catch us now, won't they?"

"They'll try."

Fargo pulled her up behind him and they were in motion once more. He swung due west this time, toward the setting sun, riding up out of the basin. A glance to the northeast revealed bobbling specks on the horizon. The Jefferses were gaining. Everything depended on whether Fargo could stay ahead of them until nightfall.

The Ovaro had seldom let Fargo down, and in this instance the stallion dipped into its remarkable reservoir of stamina and maintained a steady gallop longer than Fargo would have thought possible. Still, the specks became stick figures, the stick figures grew in size and clarity until Fargo could see belt buckles and spurs and cartridge belts glittering in the rays of the steadily sinking sun. The killers weren't in rifle range yet, but they soon would be.

A range of hills appeared ahead, so near, yet so far. Fargo could tell the Ovaro was tiring rapidly. He didn't whip it with the reins or apply his spurs. The stallion was giving its all and could give no more.

At length the sun was gone. Welcome darkness spread over the prairie like a great black veil, bringing with it cooler temperatures, a brisk breeze, and for Fargo and Lorraine the promise of a few more hours of life. They galloped in among the hills and Fargo cut to the right, around the base of the first one. He stopped in a spray of dirt and grass among shrub trees and bent low, pulling Lorraine down against him. She had no need to ask why.

Not a minute later the outlaws thundered past the hill, just so many inky silhouettes against the backdrop of night. They pounded westward, never slowing.

Fargo did not straighten until the hoofbeats waned with distance. He rode back to the point where they had entered the hills and turned northward toward the trail to Ripclaw, walking the pinto. For the first time all day they were safe, yet only for a while. Eventually Homer and his kin would recognize they had been outwitted. And what then? Fargo reflected. Would they scour the hills or go on to Ripclaw?

"Pretty slick, Skye," Lorraine Knobel commented. "Another few seconds and they would have had us."

"We're not out of the woods yet," Fargo reminded her.

"I'm not worried. You're better than they are. You'll see us safely through."

Fargo would have liked to share her confidence. The men—

and woman—they were up against would as soon shoot them in the back as look at them. He never knew when the next attack might come, when an ambush might be sprung. And even if he eluded the Jefferses, he couldn't simply up and leave Texas. They were bound to hunt Lorraine down to keep her from testifying in court. He couldn't allow that to happen.

About ten o'clock Fargo came on a patch of forest covering several hills. A clearing a hundred yards in gave him a place to call a halt. He unsaddled the stallion and laid out his blankets. Lorraine was asleep as soon as her head sank down. He stayed awake a while longer, listening and thinking ahead to Ripclaw. Intuition told him the final showdown with the Jefferses clan would take place there. One way or the other, their reign of terror was going to end.

14

"It looks peaceful enough," Lorraine Knobel remarked as she scanned their destination from a low hill half a mile to the southeast.

"We can't really tell from here," Fargo said, doing the same. It was the middle of the afternoon, and after days of arduous travel they had finally reached Ripclaw in one piece. Much to his surprise, they hadn't seen any sign of the outlaws, and that in itself led him to believe the killers had something special planned, a surefire trap from which they couldn't escape. There hadn't even been any recent tracks—at least none left by a large group of riders. So either the killers had split up into small groups to enter the town without drawing suspicion, or they were lying in wait somewhere outside Ripclaw, somewhere where they could command a clear view of the roads and trails leading into it.

"Do we sit here all day?" Lorraine asked impatiently. "I can't wait to sink into a hot tub laced with lilac and soak for hours."

"Would you rather be clean or dead?" Fargo responded. But she had a point. They had sat there for thirty minutes and not seen a thing out of the ordinary. The Sharps in his right hand, he trotted down the hill and into a strip of brush that ended a few hundred feet from Ripclaw's outskirts.

Lorraine's hand touched the back of his neck. "No matter what happens today, I want you to know I'm grateful for all you've done for me. And I'll do whatever it takes to help clear your name."

"I'm obliged."

"Is that all?"

"Don't start again," Fargo said. For the past two days she had dropped hints that she would like him to stick around once the Jeffers business was finished. She'd mentioned five or six times how nice it would be if she had someone to help run the boardinghouse, how the job was too much for a single person. He knew the signs all too well. Ordinarily, by now he would have been halfway to Denver. This time he had a debt to settle first.

At the end of the brush Fargo drew rein. From where he sat, he could see a side street and a short stretch of the main street. People were moving about as they normally did. There were children playing, horses at hitch rails.

"Seems fine to me," Lorraine nagged.

"Not yet," Fargo said, still not convinced. He studied the roofs, the alleys, any shadows where an assassin might lurk in ambush.

"Maybe you're content to sit in this hot sun the rest of the day, but I'm not," Lorraine held her ground. "I'll go in by myself, if that's how it has to be."

Fargo walked the Ovaro forward, into the side street and down to the junction with Main. He looked both ways. Men and women strolled to and fro on both sides. An old matron was crossing with the help of a young boy. A dog scratched itself in front of a saloon. Ripclaw was as peaceful as any other small town, and yet a persistent feeling that it was somehow different than it should be gnawed at him.

"Come on, will you?" Lorraine goaded. "I don't want everyone to see me looking such a sorry sight."

Fargo saw the marshal's office and made toward it, riding in the middle of the street in case they were attacked from either side. The many citizens strolling about hardly even glanced at them, which he thought a trifle odd. Strangers always attracted notice and were cause for gossip around the supper table. He drew within a dozen feet of the hitching post in front of the marshal's when another odd fact occurred to him. There were an awful lot of people up and around for that time of the day— two or three times as many as there should be.

Marshal Lee Howes suddenly filled the doorway to his office. By rights the lawman should have gone for his gun and ordered Fargo to throw up his hands. Yet Howes merely smiled a sickly sort of smile while his eyes blinked ten times in ten seconds and his mouth twitched to the right as if he were having a fit.

Bewildered, Fargo reined up. Lorraine slipped off before he could stop her. He went to dismount and his gaze fell on the lawman's holster, which was empty. At the same moment, men dashed around both corners of the building, their revolvers out and trained on him, and from within rose a harsh cackle he knew all too well, mixed with female laughter.

Marshal Howes was shoved from behind and stumbled onto the boardwalk. From out of his office filed Homer and Cassandra Jeffers, followed by the two men Fargo had passed on the trail, the undertaker-type and the young man in the black vest.

All activity on the street had stopped. Everyone stood frozen, watching in helpless frustration or fear.

Lorraine screamed and turned to flee. One of the gunmen caught her by the wrist and roughly pushed her to the ground. She went to rise but he raised a hand, threatening to strike her if she did.

Fargo sat perfectly still the whole time, his hands on the saddlehorn. With three cocked pistols fixed on his chest, there was nothing else he could do. He had expected a trap, but nothing this elaborate, this brazen. Homer Jeffers sneered at him and walked up to the Ovaro.

"Fancy meeting you here," the brains of the outlaw family gloated. "And it sure did take you long enough! We've been waiting a whole day, keeping the good marshal company."

Marshal Howes had his huge fists bunched and was ready to pounce. "Go to hell, you son of a bitch! If it's the last thing I ever do, I'll see that you swing for this!"

"I reckon you would," Homer said, unperturbed. "But we don't intend to stick around long enough to be invited to a necktie social. We've decided things are a mite too hot for us in Texas, so we're fixing to head for friendlier parts."

Cassandra ambled over. "After we take care of some unfinished business," she said, laying a hand on the stallion. She grinned at Fargo, then transferred her hand to his leg. "My brothers have promised I can have first crack at you. I can't make up my mind whether to take a bullwhip to your hide or chop off your fingers one by one."

Fargo made no reply. He was not about to do anything that would earn him a bullet in the gut. The marshal, however, had no such concern. Howes strode into the street and bellowed at the people.

"What is the matter with you? You can't just stand there and let this happen! You have to rise up against these vermin! Do something!"

Homer snickered and shook his head. "They won't lift a finger, lawman, not when they know we'll fill you full of lead if anyone so much as gives us sass. Why do you think we paid you a visit as soon as we hit town? Because we're partial to your company?"

Fargo had listened to that strident laugh again. All the outlaws joined in, he noted, except for the pair from the trail. They never smiled, never showed any emotion. Like matching bookends, they stood on either side of a post, their thumbs hooked in their gun belts, their cold eyes never still for a moment. He knew beyond a shadow of a doubt that they were two of the deadliest men he had ever run into.

Marshal Howes looked at him. "Sorry, Fargo. I wanted to warn you off, but they had a gun to my back and said they'd start shooting passersby if I did anything."

Fargo nodded at Homer. "Did this one tell you I'm not to blame for those killings in Kingfish?"

"Not in so many words," Howes said, "but I've guessed as much." He faced Homer and the redhead. "You're plumb crazy if you think you can pull this off and live long enough to reach the border. Every lawman this side of the Pecos will be on your trail once I spread the word."

"If you were to spread it before we pull out, yes, they would," Homer amended. "But we're thinking of taking you along, after letting the good people of your town know that if we see a single badge before we reach Missouri, they'll have to find themselves a new marshal."

Fargo had never met anyone as boldly reckless as the Jeffers family. No one else would have dared hold an entire town at bay by taking a town lawman hostage. It was a ruthless act, in keeping with all the other daring crimes they had committed in their violent careers. Frank and Bob had taken all the credit, but as Fargo now knew, Homer and Cassandra deserved equal blame—if not more. The four of them were like peas in a pod, as close-knit as any family could be. Or were they? He glanced at the pair of killers and said, "Aren't you going to introduce me, Homer?"

Homer tilted his head. "That's right. You haven't met my brothers yet." He pointed at the undertaker. "That there is Frank, the oldest. Slickest man with a six-shooter you ever will see. And Bob is no slouch, either."

"They must be proud of the way you helped them out by having me blamed for those murders," Fargo mentioned.

"Shucks. They'd do the same for me," Homer said with false humility.

"Was it their idea or yours to pick the Knobels? Pretty clever, since everyone knew they had thousands of dollars stashed in their house," Fargo said.

Homer jerked. "What?"

"What are you going to do with your share?" Fargo asked. "Buy a new spread in Missouri?"

Cassandra had turned toward Homer. "You never mentioned anything about any money. Are you holding out on us, older brother, dear?"

"Never!" Homer said shrilly. "He's up to something. You can't believe a word the bastard says."

"Why would I lie?" Fargo challenged, and looked at Lorraine. Everything depended on whether she was quick-witted enough to play along. "Tell them about the money your folks had saved," he said, and wanted to kiss her when she answered without hesitation.

"It was about six thousand. Turned up missing after they were killed. Every last penny we had."

Cassandra, Frank, and Bob stared at Homer. So did the four gunmen. Homer shifted from foot to foot and held out his hands, palms up. "There isn't a lick of truth to anything they're saying, damn it! I never stole any money. And if I had, I'd know better than to double-deal any of you. We always split four ways. No exceptions."

"I wonder," Cassandra said suspiciously. "We've had to warn you before about taking more than your share."

"A few dollars here and there, maybe," Homer said, "but I'd never outright cheat you."

Frank Jeffers suddenly stepped off the boardwalk, snake-swift in his movements. "We're leaving," he declared, and two of the gunmen ran to a hitching post and began collecting horses. Frank strode to the center of Main Street, hands on his Colts. "Anyone trails us, your marshal dies," he called out. "Anyone leaves town before we're out of sight, your marshal dies. And don't think of sending a wire. We've already cut the lines."

Some of the men listening fingered their guns. It was clear many itched to come to the lawman's aid but were unwilling to endanger his life.

Bob Jeffers now moved, as fluidly as his brother. He walked up to the Ovaro and fixed rattler eyes on Fargo. "We'll pry the truth out of Homer. And if you and the woman are lying, I'm going to show you an Apache trick I picked up. You'll scream for days."

The outlaws' horses were produced. Mounts were also brought for Lorraine and Marshal Howes, animals belonging to townsmen. Howes balked until a revolver was poked in his ribs. Frank and Bob then took the lead and galloped northward out of Ripclaw, scattering those on the sidewalks with a flurry of gunshots that broke a half-dozen windows.

Fargo had his pistol and rifle taken before they rode out. He galloped alongside Lorraine, the lawman right behind them. On either hand were gunmen, to the rear Cassandra and Homer, arguing fiercely. His ruse had worked far better than he had hoped, but now he must come up with another brain-storm before the killers called a halt and had them bound.

For the moment the killers were solely interested in putting as many miles behind them as they could. Frank and Bob rode as men long accustomed to the saddle, their hands never far from their revolvers. The younger one, Bob, showed an inter-est in Lorraine. He glanced at her frequently, wearing the look of a cat about to devour prey.

Fargo had been lucky in one respect. Cassandra had not

thought to mention his toothpick, which she had seen him use on several occasions. She was too busy spatting with Homer over the money. Once they stopped squabbling, she was sure to remember.

The road climbed for a while into more hills, then slowly wound down into verdant bottomland. Now and again they came on travelers, who moved aside to let them pass. Two hours out of Ripclaw they had to make way themselves for a stage barreling south. The driver waved at Marshal Howes.

Fargo thought of a plan to turn the tables, but its success depended on how fond Frank and Bob were of Cassandra, and on being able to draw the toothpick unseen. He waited for a chance that never came, and presently a pond appeared ahead and they slowed. Soon they would stop to water the horses and it would be too late.

Fargo shifted the reins to his left hand and dangled his right, shaking it as if he were relieving a kink. At the same time he slid his boot partway out of the stirrup and held his leg so that the top of the boot was within inches of his fingers. He heard Cassandra curse Homer, and glanced back to see her pull in front of her brother and make as if to pass him on the right.

Fargo touched the edge of his boot, then slowly slid his fingers underneath. The hilt was right where it should be. He hadn't taken his eyes off Cassandra, who glanced at him and frowned, her gaze straying downward as she drew next to him. He saw her stare at his hand in the boot and knew she had realized her mistake. Her head shot up and she opened her mouth to shout.

Streaking the knife out, Fargo twisted, seized Cassandra around the waist, and swung her onto the Ovaro. The gunmen went for their pistols, but before a shot could ring out Fargo had jabbed the tip of the toothpick so deeply into Cassandra's throat that she screeched in pain and fear. The gunmen hesitated, fearful of hitting her, and everyone halted.

Frank and Bob had wheeled at the scream. Six-shooters blossomed as if by magic in their hands. But they, too, hesitated.

"With my dying breath I'll kill her!" Fargo declared, trying to keep all the gunmen and Frank and Bob and Homer in sight at once. Homer was the only one who hadn't gone for his gun.

Bob Jeffers wore a nasty grin. "I can do it, Frank," he said. "Right between the eyes before he moves a muscle."

"And if he stabs just as you shoot?" Frank responded. "I've seen men who were dead on their feet keep moving out of sheer reflex, just chickens with their heads cut off. No gunplay unless I say so. Think of sis."

"It's her own stupid fault for getting too close to him."

"No, and that's final."

Fargo strained to keep his grip on Cassandra. Only her left leg was on the Ovaro. He supported most of her weight with his one arm, and it was tiring rapidly. Digging the toothpick in a bit deeper to prevent her from trying anything, he pulled her closer, onto the saddle. "I want all of you to drop your guns," he commanded.

"Never happen, mister," Frank Jeffers said coolly. "No one takes my pistols from me. Ever."

"The same here," Bob said. "And it won't matter if you carve into sissy or not. The only way anyone will get my guns is if they're pried from my stiff fingers."

Fargo was in a bind. It had never occurred to him the brothers would be more attached to their hardware than their own sister. He'd counted on them caring enough for Cassandra to lay down their six-shooters without a fuss. "Then I want you to holster your guns and back off," he said.

"Why should we, when all we have to do is wait you out?" Frank said. "You're not going anywhere, surrounded as you are. Sooner or later you'll lower that knife and we'll finish this."

"Yep," Bob chimed in. "Besides, I don't think you have the gumption to cut a woman. It takes a special knack. I know, because I've cut a few in my time."

Fargo had no idea what to do next. They held all the cards. If he stabbed Cassandra, they'd shoot him. If he didn't stab Cassandra, if he dropped his arm, they'd shoot him anyway. His plan had worked against him. It seemed hopeless. And then, out of the corner of his eyes, he saw Marshal Lee Howes moving slowly forward on the left. The gunmen never noticed.

They were riveted on his arm, waiting to see what he would do.

The marshal suddenly rammed his spurs into his mount, causing the startled animal to take a bound that brought it, in a flash, alongside one of the gunmen. The killer tried to turn to confront Howes but the huge lawman was too fast for him. Howes scooped the hardcase out of the saddle as handily as Fargo had grabbed Cassandra, then kept on going, holding the gunman in front of him like a living shield.

Howes bore down at a gallop on Frank and Bob Jeffers. Frank Jeffers instantly swerved aside. So did Bob, but as he moved, he fired his right-hand Colt three times. Two crimson holes blossomed on the gunman's chest, one on the lawman's arm. A lesser man would have fallen. Lee Howes hurled the dead killer into Bob Jeffers, and both went down.

While this took place, Fargo was also in motion. He reined the Ovaro to the left and plunged into the brush bordering the road, holding tight to Cassandra since she was his insurance the gunmen wouldn't fire.

"Lorraine! This way!" Fargo yelled, and glanced back as the vegetation closed around him. Lorraine's horse hugged the Ovaro's tail. He also saw Marshal Howes fleeing northward, saw Howes sway in the saddle as Frank Jeffers fired twice. Then branches blocked his view and he had no idea whether Howes lived or died.

Bullets ripped through the foliage, both above and below. Fargo angled to the right, then the left. He could hear Frank Jeffers roaring in fury.

"Don't just sit there, you jackasses! He's got our sister. Get after them!"

Fargo found it impossible to hold onto the redhead and guide the stallion at the same time, so he dumped Cassandra, letting go as he swept by a patch of prickly thistles. She squawked when her backside hit, then leaped erect as if someone had set her fanny on fire.

Fargo ducked under a tree limb and veered to the right again. Lorraine kept pace, hunched over her horse. Slugs chased them at random, clipping limbs, trunks, and leaves. Fargo guessed that the three surviving hired guns were after them—possibly Homer, too. Somehow he must lose them, which was easier contemplated than done. The killers were too close, coming on too rapidly.

A knoll bloomed ahead. Fargo went up to the near slope in a rush, the earth around the pinto spewing dirt. He swept over the top and was nearly unhorsed by a low, slender limb. At the last moment he threw out an arm, pushing the limb backward. It snapped off in his hand. He raced past several more trees, then swung around a thicket. Reining up, he motioned for Lorraine to continue on. She did, giving him a quizzical look.

Fargo grasped the limb firmly. The drum of hooves was almost upon him. He turned and saw the foremost gunman race around the thicket. The man saw him but was unable to stop or employ his six-gun in time. Fargo swung the limb in a tight arc and caught the gunman full in the mouth. Something crunched, and the killer went flying into the path of his companions.

Fargo threw down the limb and hastened after Lorraine. There were curses and whinnies to his rear, and he grinned at the confusion he had caused. It would buy him thirty precious seconds.

The bottomland became dense with brambles. Fargo plowed through a berry patch and saw Lorraine slowing down beyond. He motioned for her to keep going, but stubbornly she ignored him and waited for him to catch up.

"I won't desert you," she said before he could get a word out of his mouth.

Fargo did not bother arguing. He jumped off the stallion and handed her the reins. "Ride like hell," he said, "and don't stop until you're sure no one is after you."

"But what about you?"

"I need a gun, and there's only one way to get one. Now go." Fargo took off his hat and shooed her horse as she reluctantly obeyed. He ducked down into the brambles, heedless of the many thorns that tore at his clothing and flesh. Clasping the toothpick in his right hand, he tensed, listening to the approach of riders—two at least, possibly three. They were following the trail of crushed vegetation, and would pass within several feet of his hiding place.

A shadow appeared, the shape of a horse and man flitting

across the brambles like a disembodied spirit. Fargo peered through the tiny branches and saw the lead gunman, a pudgy tough who favored a Remington and was staring in the direction Lorraine had gone, not down at the ground.

"I see them!" the killer declared. "No, wait! I think it's just the woman, leading his horse. Where the hell is he?"

Fargo provided the answer by bursting from concealment and leaping onto the gunman. He streaked his throwing knife into the rider's chest, twice in swift succession. The man was dead before he realized what had happened. The Remington started to slip from his slack fingers and Fargo plucked it loose and whirled.

The second gunman had his own pistol leveled. He banged a shot, rushing it, and missed. Fargo thumbed off two shots of his own, and didn't. The killer flipped rearward, landing headfirst in the brambles. His legs kicked a few times, then he was still.

Fargo vaulted onto the first rider's horse, a calico that responded nicely to his handling of the reins. For the moment Lorraine was safe. Marshal Howes, though, might be wounded, lying on the road in need of help. So it was toward the road he flew, alert for the clan of cutthroats.

Cassandra came into sight first, riding double with the man Fargo had smashed in the mouth, heading toward the road. She looked back, gaped in amazement, and said something to the rider. He was young—so young he had fuzz on his chin instead of whiskers. He clawed at the pistol in his holster while wheeling his mount.

Fargo snapped off a shot that caught the young killer in the temple. The gunman's own gun went off a second later, into the head of his horse, and the animal reared, pawing at the sky as blood spurted from its skull.

Cassandra cried out, tried to snatch the reins as she began sliding backward, and failed. She hit the ground hard, the rider falling on top of her. Frantically she pushed and kicked, trying to shove him off. A shadow fell across her upturned face just as she did, and she glanced up in dawning horror as the stricken horse fell. It had reared so far back that it toppled straight backwards. It fell on top of her.

Fargo was ten feet away. The snap and crackle of breaking

bones raised goosebumps on his skin. He slowed and glimpsed Cassandra's head jutting out from under the animal's neck. Her blank eyes were wide, her mouth open in the scream she had never voiced. One down, Fargo reflected, three to go. He galloped faster and soon came to the road. It was deserted save for the horse of the gunman Lee Howes had used as a shield, and the gunman's body, facedown. The marshal was gone. Homer, Frank, and Bob were nowhere in sight.

Wary of a trick, Fargo trotted up to the horse. Its rider had been the one who disarmed him back in Ripclaw, and the barrel of the Sharps poked from the dead man's bedroll. Fargo quickly yanked the rifle out. A check on the man's saddlebags turned up the Colt. Smiling grimly, he verified both weapons were loaded, shoved the Colt in his holster, and sped down the road to the next bend.

Fargo swept around the curve, the Sharps to his shoulder. Two hundred yards away Lee Howes had finally fallen. Standing over him, brutally kicking him again and again, were Frank and Bob Jeffers. Halfway between them and the bend was Homer, on his way back, apparently to make certain their hired guns had taken care of Fargo and Lorraine.

Homer Jeffers was caught completely off guard. He gawked at Fargo as if seeing a ghost. Then he raised the pistol in his right hand, taking precise aim. Unlike his younger brothers, he wasn't a gunman. It proved his undoing.

Fargo had seldom felt as much satisfaction on stroking the trigger as he did now. He saw the top of Homer's head explode but had little time to watch Homer ooze from the saddle. Frank and Bob Jeffers had looked up on hearing the gunshot and were already dashing for their horses. Expecting them to pull out rifles and blaze away, Fargo commenced reloading, his fingers flying.

The two killers reached their mounts. Yet instead of resorting to rifles, they jumped on their horses and sped off up the road.

Fargo didn't know what to make of it. They were ruthless killers, not errant cowards. Fleeing made no sense. He was torn between giving chase and checking to see if Lee Howes was alive. Then the lawman moved, and Fargo lowered the Sharps and rode to the marshal.

Howes had been shot four times, twice in the arm, twice high in the chest. He had suffered a terrible beating, his face split in places and bleeding profusely. Incredibly, he was still alive, his eyes open as Fargo ran to him.

"Lie still. I'll send Lorraine for a doctor as soon as she gets here."

"No," Howes croaked. "Get them."

Fargo put a hand on the lawman's shoulder. "You come first. A posse will go after them as soon as the word spreads."

"No posse!" the marshal spat. "Posses always fail! You go, Fargo. Catch them. Kill the bastards!"

"And what about you?"

"I look worse than I am. I don't think they hit my lungs. And I've been beaten worse than this before. Don't worry about me, damn it!"

Fargo glanced after the fleeing pair, who were four hundred yards distant.

"Think about all the innocent folks they've killed," Howes said. "Think of all those they will kill if you don't stop them, here and now." He clutched at Fargo's arm, pleading, "Please! No one will ever have a better chance." Howes paused, gasped, "*They always use pistols. Do you understand? Pistols!*"

The Ovaro took off the moment Fargo's foot hit the stirrup. At a breakneck gallop he pursued the terrors of Texas. He did indeed understand, and marveled that he hadn't seen the truth sooner. Seldom was a person equally proficient with a revolver and a rifle. Being a marksman with a rifle did not automatically mean a man would be a marksman with a six-shooter, or the other way around. A man might be exceptional with one, poor with the other. The two required different skills. There was more to using them than simply aiming and hoping for the best.

Frank and Bob Jeffers were excellent pistol shots, as they had demonstrated time and again. Both had probably spent countless hours practicing to become as good as they were. But as Marshal Howes had noted, they seldom relied on rifles. Pistols were all they had ever needed. Pistols had seen them through trouble time and again. So it was likely that neither was more than a middling rifle shot.

Skye Fargo was one of the best. On the open prairie he had dropped buffalo at hundreds of yards. In shooting contests he had won top prize every time except once. If he could overtake the killers, he could put an end to their bloody careers. Bending to the task, he spurred the Ovaro on.

A quarter of a mile to the north the road rose to the top of a hill. Frank and Bob were fifty yards from the crest. Bob looked back, and even at that range his smirk was obvious.

Fargo never slackened his pace. He watched the two pass over the hill and imagined them thinking they were safe. By the time he reached the summit they were hundreds of yards down the slope. Abruptly reining up, he slid off and walked to a level spot. He swiveled the rear sight up, then studied the lay of the road. Wetting a finger, he tested the air, gauging the wind speed and direction.

Bob Jeffers straightened and laughed, waving his hat, confident they were safe. Twisting, he looked back.

Fargo pressed the stock to his shoulder and made a last adjustment on the sight. He took his time aiming. The shot rolled off across the bottomland toward a pristine river, and at the retort Bob Jeffers left his saddle and bounced twice.

Frank Jeffers could have gone on, but he stopped. He rode to his brother, stared at Bob a moment, then drew both pistols, turned his horse, and galloped toward the hill. He began firing, but not wildly. He squeezed off a shot every five or ten seconds, aiming carefully each time.

The first slug ripped into the ground dozens of yards short of where Fargo stood. He advanced slowly, reloading. The next three shots all fell well short, but the fourth kicked up dirt within ten feet of his boot tips. Fargo lifted the Sharps again, sighted down the barrel, then paused. A slug clipped a clod of dirt inches from his legs. Another buzzed past his head. The Sharps boomed, at long last, and Frank Jeffers joined his brother in the dust.

Fargo slowly lowered his rifle and walked to the Ovaro. He climbed on, looked once at the men who had caused him so much hardship, then headed off to help the wounded lawman and get his life back in order.

LOOKING FORWARD!
The following is the opening
section from the next novel in the exciting
Trailsman **series from Signet:**

THE TRAILSMAN #159
NORTH COUNTRY GUNS

1861, east of White Bear and west
of Moose Jaw, the province of Saskatchewan
in the wild, untamed land called Canada,
where the only law was lawlessness . . .

It was nearing the end of the day when the big man with the lake-blue eyes heard the screams as he rode through the forest of balsam fir and white spruce. Skye Fargo reined the magnificent Ovaro to a halt as the screams came again—women's voices first, then children's, and finally the coarse cries of men. He turned the horse down the slope to his left, skirting the closely packed tree trunks, and when he reached the bottom of the slope he emerged from the forest to see the river in front of him. Two wagons, nondescript, makeshift rigs with canvas tops, were on the other side, and most of their occupants were already strewn across the ground. Yet a furious battle still raged. More than a half-dozen fiercely whooping Indians attacked a lone figure against one of the wagons, a man wearing some sort of uniform with a brilliant scarlet jacket and a Sam Browne belt, black jodhpurs and a wide-brimmed hat with a high peak pinched in at the top.

He was putting up a fierce fight with a pistol and rifle, and two more of his attackers lay on the ground, Fargo saw; but he had dropped to one knee with three arrows in him—two in one leg and a third in his shoulder. There were just too many for the lone figure, and Fargo saw one of the Indians send another arrow into the man as the others rushed to close in. "Damn," Fargo spit out as out of the corner of one eye he saw two more Indians still smashing their tomahawks into the bodies strewn across the riverbank. Fording the river in the face of the attack would make him a near-helpless target in midstream, he realized, and he sent the Ovaro racing twenty yards down the bank before turning the horse into the water. The river proved deep and the pinto had to swim most of the way. When he emerged on the other bank, he saw the scarlet-jacketed figure lying prone on the ground, yet still fighting off the blows of his attackers. Fargo drew the big Colt from its holster as he raced the horse toward the wagons, his first object to stop the attackers from killing their victim. He fired off three shots at a full gallop.

Two of the Indians went down and four others turned to see him charging at them. They scooped up bows, and Fargo flattened himself in the saddle as a flurry of arrows sailed toward him. Two rifle shots followed the arrows, and with one quick motion Fargo spun the Ovaro in a tight circle and dove from the saddle on the side away from the Indians. Only a narrow strip of open ground lay between the riverbank and the line of trees. He hit the ground already rolling. He continued to roll toward the trees as he fired off another shot and felt two arrows thud into the soft earth near him. He twisted as he rolled, half dived, and an arrow grazed his leg, but he reached the line of trees and flung himself into the brush. He rolled again, half rose, and dived into a dense thicket of tall fireweed, where he lay motionless on his stomach.

He could peer through the tall brush to see the four Indians move into the trees to search for him. They moved slowly shadowy shapes in the dimness of the forest and the gathering dusk. They had their short bows drawn, arrows in place on bowstrings, ready to hurl through the air. Fargo's finger rested against the trigger of the big Colt. Once he fired they'd know where he was, he thought in grim silence. He had to make his first shots count. Hardly daring to breathe, he watched the four searchers move closer, and he waited another dozen precious seconds. One of the Indians moved half behind the figure in front of him. It was the best moment he'd find, Fargo decided, and he raised the Colt as he tensed every muscle of his body. When he pressed the trigger the two shots sounded almost as one, and the first Indian crumpled instantly, the man half behind him doubling in two as the second shot tore through his abdomen.

But Fargo was already flinging himself sideways as the other two Indians loosed their arrows. He felt one shaft graze his leg as the arrows slammed into the thicket where he'd been. They heard him rolling through the brush and followed with another volley of arrows. Fargo fired a shot as he rolled, not taking enough time to aim, and missed. Both pursuers were almost upon him. He pushed to one knee but had to drop flat to avoid an arrow fired at point-blank range. He glanced up to glimpse the tomahawk coming at him, tried to twist away but the side of the tomahawk slammed into his right forearm. He felt the revolver drop from his hand as his fingers went numb, and he fell on his back as he saw the figure diving at him. He managed to get one knee up and let it slam into the man's belly, heard the Indian's gasp of pain, but the attacker still landed atop him. The man's hands reached to circle his throat, but Fargo felt the numbness fade from his own hand and brought his fist around in a short blow that smashed into the side of his attacker's face.

Though awkwardly thrown, the blow was hard enough to knock the Indian half off him. Fargo was about to push to his feet when he saw the fourth Indian with his bow drawn, waiting for a chance to fire his arrow. Fargo flung himself across the Indian beside him, pulling the man with him as he rolled.

The Indian tried to twist away but Fargo clung to him as a wet leaf clings to a rock, rolling again with his arms wrapped around his foe. The Indian with the drawn bow followed, still trying to get a closer shot. The red man in Fargo's grip cursed, managed to get one arm free, and brought his hand, fingers outstretched, to jab into his eyes. Fargo turned his head in time to take the stiff-fingered jabbing blow against his temple. Using his superior strength, yet keeping his hold of the smaller Indian, he pushed himself upwards, taking the man with him. On his feet, head pushed into the Indian's chest and arms wrapped around him, Fargo swung himself in a half circle, exposing himself to the waiting archer. Out of the corner of his eye, he saw the man take a split second to pull his bowstring back a fraction further, and then the arrow flew through the air. Fargo waited his own split second before whirling again with the man in his grasp. He felt the man's body stiffen as the arrow hurtled into the small of his back.

Unwrapping his arms from the man, he charged forward, knocking aside the falling figure with the arrow almost entirely through his body, to bowl into the other Indian as he tried to fix another arrow into his bowstring. The Indian went down sideways, the arrow falling aside, but he clung to the bow. He hit the ground on one knee and as Fargo came after him he rose and, using the end of the bow as a spear, thrust it forward with a lunge. Fargo managed to pull his head back as he half twisted, and the bow end all but brushed his face. He sunk a powerful, hooking blow into the Indian's side and felt the snap of one rib as the man cried out in pain. A left cross followed that landed on the man's jaw and the Indian went down, rolled, but not fast enough to avoid Fargo's knees as they landed atop his spine. He let out a garbled cry of anguish as his vertebrae snapped. As Fargo pushed to his feet, the man's body twitched convulsively and his hands clasped and unclasped until he finally lay still.

Fargo spun, spied the Colt in the grass and scooped it up, dropped to one knee, listening. There had been two more Indians by the bodies of the slain travelers, but he heard only silence now. They had fled, he thought as he rose to his feet and hurried from the trees to the narrow strip of land along the riverbank. He ran to where the scarlet-jacketed figure lay alongside one of the wagons, dropped down beside the man and saw he was somehow still alive, though bleeding from a dozen wounds. "No, don't try to talk," Fargo said as the man attempted to gasp out a word. Fargo whistled and the Ovaro trotted over. Fargo rose and dug into his saddlebag to find a roll of cloth-bandage strips.

He had just dropped down to the barely alive figure when he heard the sound in the trees. He rose instantly, positioned himself at the edge of the wagon, his eyes on the tree line. A voice called out—a woman's voice. "Don't shoot," it said, and Fargo watched as a short-legged horse and its rider emerged from the junipers. He stepped from behind the wagon, but kept the Colt in his hand as he watched the horse draw nearer and come to a halt. A young woman, bare-armed in a leather vest and a fringed deerskin skirt that encircled a slender shape, swung from the horse and rushed to the uniformed figure. "Good God, he's still alive," she said.

"Just about," Fargo said.

She leaned over the man. "Thomas, can you hear me?" she asked, and the man managed to move his head. "Hold on. Just you hold on," she said. "We'll get you to a doctor." She lifted her face to Fargo. "I'll help you with the bandages. Sit him up so we can get his jacket off," she said. She rose, went to the pack on her horse as Fargo holstered the Colt, and returned with a leather-covered bottle. "Whiskey," she said, and after they had the man sitting up and his jacket off, she managed to get some of the liquid down his throat. Fargo's eyes went over the man's body.

"We can only bandage the worst of his wounds," he said grimly, and she nodded and began to use a cloth to wipe some of the blood from the man's body. She worked quickly and deftly beside him as he bandaged the deepest wounds, Fargo noted, and he had a chance to look at her again. There was Indian blood in her, he decided. It was in the high-cheekboned contours of her face, in the hint of olive in her skin, and in the slight flare of her nostrils and the thin black eyebrows. It was also in the cool, unflustered gaze she gave him, a kind of pride that bore its own regal stamp. But her eyes were hazel and her long hair, held by a pin at her back, had a tinge of red in it.

"Talk to me while we work," Fargo said. "Who is he?"

"Officer Thomas Moran of the Northwest Mounted Police," she said.

"Who are they? Never heard of them." Fargo frowned.

"I imagine you will in time," she said.

"You were with him?" Fargo questioned.

"Yes," she said.

"Who are you?" Fargo asked.

"Lisette Dumas," she answered. "I was hired as a guide for Officer Moran. I know this country very well."

He hesitated a moment as he tightened a bandage and then decided to go on. "What tribe?" he slid at her, his glance quick, and he saw her hazel eyes turn on him, a moment of cool appraisal, and then a half smile touched her lips.

"You're very quick. My hair and eyes fool most people," she said.

"I get paid to see what most people don't see," Fargo told her.

She held the half smile as she continued to study his strong, chiseled face. "My mother was Sekani, my father was a French trapper. I used to help him work his trap lines. When he died, I got work as a guide," she said. "You're not Canadian," she added, the half smile staying.

"That's right. American," Fargo said. "You're quick enough, too." She let the smile widen as she finished tightening the last bandage and Fargo helped her lay Thomas Moran on his side. The man was still breathing but he was unconscious—perhaps a merciful state, Fargo reflected, considering his wounds. Lisette Dumas rose and Fargo pushed to his feet with her. She was taller than he'd first observed, her legs long, smooth, and lovely, ending in narrow hips, the vest covering what seemed to be modest breasts. "Were you with the wagons?" he asked.

"No. We came onto the attack soon after it had started. We saw it from the ridge and Thomas raced down. He told me to stay in the trees. I couldn't have helped him much. I had no gun. He thought they'd run when they saw him."

"He was wrong," Fargo said as he started to make his way through the slain bodies that littered the ground. His lips drew back in disgust at the sight. Every man, every woman, and every child had been shot with arrows or bullets, stabbed with knives, and hacked with tomahawks. He paused beside two of the slain Indians and frowned down at them. "This is one of the most savage attacks I've ever seen," he said.

"Yes, even for the Cree," Lisette said.

"Is that what they were?"

"Western Cree," she said and pointed to a gunshot pouch one of the dead attackers had at his waist. "All that beadwork in flower patterns is always western Cree."

"I'll remember that," Fargo said. "One thing is plain."

"What's that?"

"They didn't want anyone left alive to talk," he said.

"Guess not. But I saw six canoes of Cree in the distance, paddling like all hell downriver," Lisette said, a tiny furrow crossing her smooth forehead.

"You think they were trying to get away, too?" Fargo questioned.

"I don't know, but it sure looked like it," Lisette said.

"You saying this was done by some pack of outlaw Cree? Renegades that everybody's afraid of?" Fargo frowned.

"I'm just telling you what I saw. I don't know what it means," she said.

Fargo grunted and cast a glance across the river. He estimated there was not more than a half hour of day left. "We haven't time to bury all these people. I'll try to find some identification on them," he said, and Lisette nodded and walked back to the unconscious figure of Thomas Moran. She was a strange admixture, he decided. In her hazel eyes he had seen the horror and pain, but her face remained composed and controlled, as though showing emotion were a weakness. Perhaps a result of the Indian half of her, he mused. He turned to his grim task and began to go through the clothing of the victims, his lips drawn back in disgust and pity. Finally he stared down at the identification he'd found in pockets and purses.

They were Americans, he found in surprise, migrating to Canada for reasons that had died with them. An unfinished letter in one woman's bag told of their excitement at becoming settlers in a new land. But that had all ended in a brief moment of vicious savagery. Shoving the pieces of identification into his pocket, he walked back to where the young woman knelt beside Thomas Moran as darkness fell.

"We've got to get him to Moose Jaw. There's a doctor there," she said.

"Moose Jaw?" Fargo exploded. "Hell, he'll never be able to ride a mile, much less to Moose Jaw. Isn't there a doctor anywhere closer?"

"No," Lisette said. "Besides, Colonel French is in Moose Jaw, too."

"Who's that?" Fargo inquired.

"His commander," Lisette said.

Fargo looked at the silent figure. The man was barely breathing. "This ride will kill him. He'll never make it," Fargo said.

"He might make it by canoe," Lisette said.

"He just might, but we don't have a canoe, honey," Fargo snapped.

"I know where we might get one," she said.

"Where?" Fargo frowned.

"There's a Cree camp about five miles downriver. Maybe we could steal a canoe," she said.

Fargo stared at her. "You're serious, aren't you?" he said.

Her chin lifted and she held almost a chiding challenge in her handsome face, the hazel eyes steady. "It's not impossible," she said.

"Only damn near so," Fargo snapped.

Lisette rested one hand on Thomas Moran's still figure. "I'd like to save his life. He's a good man. Couldn't we try?" she asked.

Fargo swore silently as he turned over her plea in his mind. "No, *we* couldn't try. If there's any chance, it'd take one person—no chance of noise, a mistake, one person sneaking into the camp alone. That's the only way it could possibly work," he said.

She glanced at him, the challenging appraisal still in the hazel eyes. "You could do it," she said. "I know you could."

"You know?" he echoed questioningly.

"Yes, something about you. I'd even bet you've done it before," she said.

He grunted and studied her as a half-moon came up. "Maybe, but that doesn't make it any less dangerous," he said.

The challenge left her eyes and her face softened as she lowered herself to the ground, folding long legs under her. "I know. It's asking a lot, more than I've a right to ask. It's just that I was taught never to turn my back on a deserving life, and Thomas Moran's is a deserving life."

Fargo lowered himself to the ground beside her as he swore under his breath. She had a simple directness that was all the more powerful because of her sincerity. He swore silently again as he spoke without looking at her. "I'll have to wait till they're asleep. That could be hours," he said, and felt her hand come to rest over his—a light, warm touch.

"Thank you," she said. "I'm very grateful to you."

"What the hell," he muttered. "Everyone's allowed a few damn fool things."

She was quiet for a moment and then her voice was soft, a sweet chiding in it. "I think it's time you told me your name," she said, and he suddenly realized the truth in her words.

"Fargo . . . Skye Fargo," he said.

"A good name . . . a very American name. I like it," she said, and somehow made it sound not unlike a regal compliment.

His eyes glanced at the still-breathing figure of Thomas Moran. "You want to tell me about him and what he was all about?" he asked.

"I'd rather Colonel French did that," she said.

"Did Moran hire you to work with him as a guide?" Fargo questioned.

"No, Colonel French did," she said.

"How long did you work with Moran?"

"Three months," she said, and he caught the sharpness of her sidelong glance. "You're wondering if I was more than a guide," she said.

Fargo half shrugged. "The thought crossed my mind," he said.

"You can uncross it. Thomas Moran was a real gentleman. He respected me. I respected him," Lisette Dumas said. "Maybe that's another reason I want to save him."

Fargo settled back against the wheel of a wagon. "I'm going to get in a nap. It's going to be a long night," he said and half closed his eyes and heard Lisette relax beside him. But even dozing refused to cooperate as the parade of thoughts marched through his mind and he found himself staring up at the half-moon as it slowly wandered across the blue-black velvet sky. He guessed an hour had gone by when Lisette's voice broke into his thoughts.

"You're not napping. You haven't napped at all. What are you thinking about?" she asked softly.

"Everything that's happened here. It wasn't an ordinary attack on a couple of wagons. Hell, I've seen enough of those. They can be vicious, but this was more than vicious. Then there were the canoes you saw paddling away. There's something more here. I don't know what, but something more," he said.

"Maybe you're right, but we can talk about that later. Right now I just want to get Thomas Moran to a doctor," she said.

Fargo glanced at the moon. Enough time had gone by. It'd take at least another hour to reach the Cree camp. He rose to his feet, reached down and pulled her up. "Come on," he grunted.

"I thought you said only one person alone had a chance." She frowned.

"Get your horse," he said, and she continued to frown as she returned with the short-legged brown gelding and swung into the saddle. Her eyes still questioned as he climbed onto the Ovaro and rode off with her. "I don't fancy walking five miles to the Cree camp and I don't fancy leaving my horse behind there," he said, and she let the frown slide from her face. He set a nice, steady canter and saw the clouds move across the moon with fitful regularity. He was grateful for that. He needed only a fitful light and no more.

Lisette rode in silence beside him and he finally slowed the pace to a walk and then drew to a halt. He took in deep draughts of the night air and picked up the smell of wood-fire embers and charred trout. "This is as far as you go," he said as he swung from the horse. "Take the Ovaro back with you and wait."

"What if you don't come back?" she asked.

"You'll have a damn fine horse to ride to Moose Jaw," he told her.

"Maybe you shouldn't try it," she murmured.

"Cold feet?"

"Something like that. I'm suddenly afraid for you and maybe ashamed at having asked you to do it," she said.

"Too late, honey. We're here now. Besides, I'd like keeping Moran alive. He may have seen something you didn't from the trees." She took the Ovaro's reins and, leaning from the saddle, placed her other hand against his cheek.

"Come back," she murmured as she drew her hand away.

"I aim to," he said and waited till she rode from sight with the two horses. He turned and, falling into a long lope of a stride, made for the Cree camp. He reached it through a line of black spruce and dropped to one knee to survey the camp. It stretched out along the riverbank. He took note of at least a dozen figures asleep on the open ground. There were certainly more in the six tipis he saw. Their tipis were not unlike the conical shape of the plains tipis, but they used many more poles—as many as twenty or more, he counted—and birch bark rather than hide outer covering.

His eyes moved along the water's edge and he saw canoes, all pulled out of the water and resting on the riverbank, as was the practice of every Indian tribe. Fargo began to edge his way round the top of the camp to the bank where, silent as a water moccasin, he slid himself into the warm river. He let the gentle current push him a few dozen yards to the first of the row of canoes, where he pulled himself from the water to lie on his stomach, his eyes scanning the camp again. There were at least four sleeping figures, all too close to the canoes, but there was nothing he could do about that. But his hand crept down to his ankle where the double-edged, thin throwing knife rested in its ankle holster. If anything went wrong he'd have only a split second to react with swiftness and silence. There'd be no time to pull his trouser leg up and draw the knife from its holster. There'd be only time to take instant aim and throw. His hand removed the thin blade from the holster and put it between his teeth as he began to crawl forward again.

He half rose at the first canoe and peered inside to be certain it held at least one paddle. He saw two and lowered himself again. Stretched out almost prone on the ground, he extended his arms to close both hands around the prow and grasp the top edges of the canoe. Working with absolute caution, he began to slide the canoe toward the water, grateful for the softness of the riverbank soil. Pausing after every few inches to glance up and survey the camp, he continued to slide the canoe forward. It was less than a half-dozen yards to the water, yet it seemed as though it were a mile. There was no weight to the canoe, yet his shoulder muscles cried out from the tensed strain of inching the vessel along silently. He was nearing the edge of the bank, about to congratulate himself on his success, when it happened. The first thing he felt was the slight shiver of the canoe under his hands, and then he heard the sound of the pebble as, dislodged, it began to roll toward the water.

It was a slight, insignificant noise, yet in the silent night it sounded to him as though it were a boulder crashing down a slope. Fargo halted in position, dropped his hands from the prow of the canoe as the pebble rolled into the water with a tiny plink that again sounded disproportionately massive. He raised his head to peer out into the camp and cursed silently as he saw the figure push itself into a sitting position not more than a few dozen yards from him. The Cree sat up and peered through the night toward him. *Shit*, Fargo muttered to himself